THORN-TREE MIDWIFE

When Staff Nurse Kate Raven takes a
post as a midwife in Central Africa, she
imagines that she has left her family
troubles behind her. So she is not best
pleased to find that handsome Dr Nicholas
Kyle of Mutala Hospital is a cousin by
marriage . . .

Books you will enjoy
in our Doctor Nurse series:

THORN-TREE
MIDWIFE

BY
BARBARA PERKINS

MILLS & BOON LIMITED
15–16 BROOK'S MEWS
LONDON W1A 1DR

*First published in Great Britain 1984
by Mills & Boon Limited*

© *Barbara Perkins 1984*
Australian copyright 1985
Philippine copyright 1985

ISBN 0 263 74933 9

Set in 10 on 11pt Linotron Times
03–0185–58,000

*Photoset by Rowland Phototypesetting Ltd
Bury St Edmunds, Suffolk
Made and printed in Great Britain by
Richard Clay (The Chaucer Press) Ltd
Bungay, Suffolk*

CHAPTER ONE

'LADIES and gentlemen, we shall be landing in Mutala in five minutes. Please fasten your seat-belts and extinguish cigarettes. Thank you. We hope you have had a good flight.'

The impersonal voice, with its faintly South African twang, brought Kate out of her reverie. She was beginning to feel as if she had been travelling for ever. Her mind told her she hadn't. Fourteen hours of flight from England to Johannesburg, an overnight stop there, then onwards for a two-hour flight in a smaller plane, scarcely qualified as eternity.

All the same it felt like it, with a dryness in her skin and a lank deadness in the heavy coil of fair hair which rested neatly on her neck. She peered downwards out of the plane window, narrowing her blue eyes against the brilliance.

She would have had to admit that the central African republic of Lanbwe didn't look all that inspiring from up here, even with her excitement to lend it glamour. It looked vast and dry—and empty. A single railway-track slashed its way across a browny-yellow landscape, dotted here and there with the merest scattering of darker-brown trees. Sometimes a lighter line suggested a dust road. The only signs of habitation were the occasional clump of round-topped huts which looked as if they had grown up suddenly in random places out of the miles of empty bush.

The sheer size of that emptiness was somehow daunting as well as intriguing. Even though Kate had known from the map how large Lanbwe was, *seeing* it was different. And this, she reminded herself, was only the

5

southern part of the country with whose government she had signed a year's contract to work as a midwife, because Lanbwe stretched twice as far again beyond Mutala, its capital, her destination.

'You *can't* go and work in the middle of Africa,' Kate's mother had wailed, when Kate had broken the news to her over the phone. '*Anything* might happen to you out there—'

'Don't be silly, Mother. Tessa's living in Mutala, and she says it's quite civilised—a lot more civilised than some of the places she's been! You remember Tessa, don't you? The girl I used to share a hospital flat with?'

'The lab technician? Didn't she go abroad on some kind of fact-finding mission?'

'Yes, that's right. She went to Africa to assist her boss on a World Health Organisation research project. We've been writing to each other ever since she left— and they've settled in Lanbwe now, and they'll be there for at least another year, she says. So you see, I shall know someone out there.'

'All the same, I don't see why *you* have to go.'

'Because it'll be interesting and it'll give me wider experience.'

Kate had no intention of giving her mother the real reason. She didn't even like to admit it to herself. Even now, when she was really here after what seemed a remarkably rushed two months of planning, she didn't like to say to herself that she had come all this way because she wanted to see Professor Richard Cranshaw again.

Even Tessa hadn't guessed that Kate carried a torch for the quiet, brilliant pathology professor who was Tessa's boss. His dedication to work had somehow seemed an ideal, and his angular form and vague manner had only seemed endearing. Tessa, working for him, had claimed to find him exasperating. But to Kate he had seemed wholly admirable.

Now, after two years, she would see him again, thanks to an article Kate had read in a newspaper saying Lanbwe was short of trained midwives, which had set her off on the enquiries which led her here. Kate, remembering the rest of her mother's reaction, felt herself flushing a little. Mrs Raven had, of course, gone on to say in alarm that Kate would be bound to meet some highly unsuitable *men* . . .

Not that her over-protective mother need have worried. Kate had been only ten when her father had left his family for another woman, but she had learned enough from that to distrust any handsome charmers such as her father had been. Nursing had helped to develop the coolly efficient manner she chose to hide behind, and it had proved a very good way of putting off approaches from the flashier type of young doctor or student who, in a large teaching hospital, was always on the look-out for a trim figure or a pretty face. No, Kate was perfectly well able to take care of herself. If her colleagues had sometimes reproached her for missing out on things, she had merely raised a polite eyebrow and said she was far too interested in her work.

Fumbling with the safety-strap to clip herself into her seat, Kate felt a tingle of excitement mixed with nervousness. She told herself firmly that she hadn't come out here *just* because Richard Cranshaw was here. He was a man she deeply admired, it was true, with his quiet good manners and his obvious brilliance and his serious cast of mind. If the slightly abstracted air he wore also made her long to look after him, that was a secret she had carefully kept.

It had been a shock when he suddenly took off for Africa to do research, taking Tessa with him as his assistant and general Girl Friday—Tessa, whose friendship had given Kate the excuse to drop in at the Pathology Department. He had been young for his professor's post, only in his thirties, and to Kate at least, the hospital certainly hadn't seemed the same without him.

Suddenly they were arriving. The plane turned in a banking curve and began to lose height steadily. Kate caught sight of what must be Mutala, a cluster of buildings, an impression of neat, low-slung squareness. The flat, bare countryside around seemed to come right up to the city's edge, and it was scarcely larger in size than an English market town.

Then it was gone again as the plane continued to turn, and a flash of bright blue below caught Kate's eye. Craning, she saw a sudden expanse of water, flat and still, with a crumpling of low hills rising out of the flatlands behind it. That must be the artificial lake known as the Dam, which Tessa had told her provided a place for picnics and sailing, though not swimming because it was also Mutala's water supply. Now the grey of an asphalt road appeared beneath them with cars scurrying along it like insects, and then the flatness resolved itself into a runway with a scattering of airport buildings around it. The wheels touched down with a soft bump.

The plane taxied to a halt and Kate gathered up her belongings. The rest of the passengers were already stirring in their seats—a mere handful of them, and mainly black faces. She felt strange and disorientated after her long journey, and even stranger as she stepped out of the plane to be dazzled by the sun, with the air smelling hot and dry and a gritty wind blowing.

It was March, so Lanbwe's summer had just ended, she reminded herself. It didn't feel like that to her, nor could she believe that the nights would be cold. Warmth soaked into her skin as she looked round eagerly, adjusting her eyes to the sunlight with its yellow haze of dust.

Mutala Airport was small, not much more than a wide open field, and her eyes searched quickly for the small, familiar, boyish-looking figure of her friend.

Tessa had promised to get time off to meet her. There was no sign of her, however, as Kate followed the rest of the passengers on the short walk across the tarmac to the one-storey, glass-fronted terminal building. Here there were black faces in neat uniforms and an air of casual efficiency—but still no sign of her friend.

Kate joined a short but steadily-moving queue, getting out her passport with its official details. Her official letter of appointment and her work permit were tucked inside it. When she reached the desk she was relieved to find the man there spoke to her in English, with merely a faintly-accented lilt. That was, she supposed, because Lanbwe had once been a British colony, and its official business was still carried out bilingually.

Now she was free to collect her luggage, two suitcases only, with her trunk following by the much slower sea route. Kate found her luggage without difficulty and glanced, frowning a little, towards the terminal's swing doors. Still no Tessa. Surely there hadn't been a mistake about the day, had there? The terminal was rapidly emptying and the only familiar face she could see was the stewardess who had flown with them—and *she* seemed thoroughly busy.

She was deep in vivacious conversation with the only other European in sight, a tall, fair man in a short-sleeved shirt which showed off his even tan, and a pair of well-cut slacks. He had a package in one hand and his head was close to the stewardess's in intimate laughter.

Kate moved restlessly, aware that he was the type who automatically made her hackles rise. He was much too handsome, with regular features above a strong jaw and that air of assurance which bespoke a man used to getting the attention of all the prettiest girls. The stewardess certainly seemed to be appreciating his company and Kate decided that she could write him off as conceited, and probably a womaniser, without even looking at him further.

She turned her back to gaze out at the quiet expanse of the airfield, with its broad tarmac and one silent plane in which she had arrived. It was somehow dispiriting not to be met and to feel that she was standing here with her luggage like a displaced person.

'Are you Miss Raven?' a deep voice asked abruptly behind her, making her jump. 'Miss Kate Raven?'

'Yes . . .?'

It was him, the man she had been watching, now giving *her* the benefit of an intent look out of a pair of dark grey eyes the disturbing colour of smoke. Kate found herself stiffening. 'Yes?' she said again, coldly.

'This isn't a pick-up, in the sense *you're* thinking,' he said drily—and disconcertingly. It was almost as if he could read her mind. 'Tessa's car's broken down, and as I had to come to the airport anyway, I said I'd meet you. I'm Nicholas Kyle.'

'Oh. Thank you.' She was disconcerted again to find herself offered a formal handshake, and aware that the firm clasp of his fingers gave her a feeling of leashed energy which was almost like an electrical charge. She drew her hand away quickly and found that he was still studying her with an unnerving intentness. He didn't seem to find it necessary to smile at her. In fact he seemed to be assessing her with a degree of grimness which made her tilt her chin even more defensively.

'My car's outside. Are these your cases? You'll have to carry one of them—I don't want to crush what's in here.' He indicated his package, picked up one of her suitcases and turned away, leaving her to follow him.

Kate, though she was perfectly capable of carrying her own suitcase, felt a surge of annoyance at his abrupt manner. He certainly didn't believe in sounding particularly welcoming, and his manner was in direct contrast to his laughter with the stewardess just now—while *she* had been left standing about waiting. She caught herself up quickly. He wasn't the type of person from whom she'd have wanted a welcome! All the same, as she followed the tall, fair-headed figure out of the terminal building, she couldn't help resenting his manner, and it reflected in the coldness of her voice as he stopped beside a grey Holden station-wagon parked outside and opened up the back to stow her cases.

'You're a friend of Tessa's? I was beginning to wonder if she'd mistaken the time I was arriving.'

'She'd hardly do that, when there's only one plane a day on the South Africa run. She rang me in a panic when her car wouldn't start. Get in the front, it's open.'

'It's kind of you to drive me,' Kate said, trying not to bring it out between her teeth. He had sounded faintly bored and she decided that he could do with a lesson in manners. 'I'm sorry if it's taking up your time.'

'No, because I had to be here anyway.' He got in beside her after stowing his package carefully on the back seat. Kate found herself annoyingly aware of him as one muscular arm almost brushed against her. She glanced round, feeling as if she should comment on the scenery, but there wasn't anything to see just here except the airport forecourt and flat scrub stretching away in the distance. As he started the motor she felt unreal, shut in a car with a slightly unnerving stranger in a completely strange country. She pulled herself together quickly, telling herself that she was only suffering from the long hours of flying.

There seemed to be an empty stretch lying between Mutala and its airport, because there were no buildings to be seen; nothing but flat scrub, yellowy-brown, coming up to the drainage ditches which edged the road. There were a few burned-looking bushes and, here and there, spindly trees with outward-spreading, thin branches looking leafless and spiny. Lanbwe, at the moment, looked no more inspiring from ground-level than it had from the air. They were driving at a steady speed, passing other cars here and there on the asphalt road, but there were no pedestrians to be seen.

Kate glanced at the silent man by her side, feeling that she ought to be asking questions—and then decided not to, and not to look as if she was studying his profile either, and turned her head sharply to look out at the scrub again. At that moment Nicholas Kyle said casually,

'Admiring the thorn trees? They're about the only wild vegetation you'll see around here at this time of year. They grow all over. More like daggers than thorns, those spikes on them, aren't they?'

'Don't they have leaves?'

'A few, if you go up close. But you won't see greenery at this time of year. It's the dry season.'

'Does Lanbwe have a wet season?'

'It can rain like a monsoon in September. Never for long enough, though. There's an overnight transformation, but then everything starts to die again. On your left you'll see the Holiday Inn, Mutala's one social centre.'

Kate turned her head at the information, but she had already seen the hotel, set back down its own tarmac road and looking somehow out of place amid the emptiness. It was built to a mere two storeys high and spread itself out sideways in a gleam of clean white paint and shining plate glass. She caught sight of a sign saying *Swimming-pool* and another saying *Casino* as they swept past. Then the scrub came back again, and she was about to ask where Mutala itself was when a sharp turn on to another asphalted thoroughfare suddenly led them among houses.

Pavements appeared each side of the road and there were drives leading to bungalows, painted in white or pastel colours under dark roofs, each house well-detached amid tidy but dried-up gardens. Kate caught flashes of colour—a mass of purple she thought might be oleanders, tall flame-orange canna lilies, something in a deep bright red—but there was still the prevailing yellow-brown dryness.

Since her companion had lapsed back into his unsociable silence, Kate felt determined not to ask him what the plants were, or how people managed gardens at all in this climate. Instead she stared out of the car window, trying not to be aware of the silent man by her side, and trying to revive her excitement and interest.

A few pedestrians seemed to be going about a typical suburban life. They were dark-skinned, but all wore European dress. It was somehow disappointing to see everything looking so ordinary. Apart from the heat and the dazzle of dust, they might have been in an English country suburb rather than in the middle of Africa. Kate opened her mouth to comment on it, glanced at the man beside her, and shut her mouth again. It was irritating that his silence made her feel defensive, particularly when he certainly wasn't someone she would have wanted to get to know. She cleared her throat, but just then he swung the car about and they seemed to be heading away from Mutala again as the houses fell behind them and scrub came back abruptly to edge the road.

'Oh, aren't we going into—'

'We're heading for Dendaa. It's a kind of expatriate village a couple of miles out of town. Built for colonial workers at one time, but now it's used for advisers and people out on contract to the Lanbwena government. Tessa was assigned a house there, and I gather you're sharing it.'

'Yes, I am.' There was really no need for him to give her information in that abrupt manner, nor to sound so unfriendly about it. Besides, though Kate had known that Tessa's address was Dendaa, there was no reason for her to have known where it was. 'I've come out here to work as a midwife,' she said stiffly, 'so I was hoping we might pass the hospital.'

'It's back that way. I'm sorry if you were expecting a conducted tour.' He didn't sound it, though he had slowed. For a moment Kate thought he was planning to turn and take her back so that she could see the place where she was to start work tomorrow, but then she realised he was merely avoiding a heavy cloud of yellow dust ahead. 'Another car on the road,' he said. 'You have to keep well back in the dry season.' And then, as they idled along, he added coolly, 'Yes, I'd gathered you were here as a midwife. Tessa told me that was your job. I hope you haven't come out expecting promotion. People straight out from England often find it hard to adjust to the fact that it isn't a colonial set-up any more. Far from it, an independent Africa! So if you were expecting to run the place, I'm afraid you'll be disappointed. Always supposing that career prospects *were* the reason you came.'

'I thought it sounded interesting, and good experience,' Kate retorted, nettled by his tone. She felt suddenly uneasy, too, at the suggestion from a total stranger that she might have had another motive in coming—a stranger who was apparently a friend of Tessa's. Surely Tessa hadn't guessed anything? 'I *have* already been told the set-up here,' she said stiffly. 'I know that I'll be a staff nurse rather than a sister because all the top jobs go to Africans, and I can assure you I don't mind that in the least! After all, straight out from London, I can't be expected to know how things are done here.'

'Just as well if you realise that,' he answered drily. Before Kate could answer, he was going on. 'If you've got the ideas people usually have when they've come straight out of a large London teaching hospital, you won't last five minutes!'

Kate was thoroughly annoyed by his dismissive tone.

She bit her lip on the inclination to ask him what *he* did here, because she wasn't going to show that much interest. All the same, she felt angry at the way he appeared to have summed her up just as quickly as she had him. She found herself hoping he was no more than an acquaintance of Tessa's and that they wouldn't see much of him.

'I don't know why you think you know so much about me, considering we've only just met,' she said icily.

To her surprise he braked sharply and turned to face her. Kate was suddenly aware of the way his deep tan accentuated the bright tow-colour of his hair and the hardness of the grey eyes fixed on her face. He said sharply, 'All right, since you've brought it up, let's have it out in the open—and then forget it, for preference! I may not have met you before today, but I certainly know of you. The name Kyle doesn't ring any bells?'

'No. Why should it? Why should you—'

'Yes, I wasn't sure if it was going to be the same Kate Raven. It did seem rather a large coincidence. However, when I saw you I was sure. Let alone the fact,' he said with a dry sarcasm, 'that you're so obviously a very uptight lady. Which is why I don't think you'll last as a nurse out here. People who can't or won't adjust to circumstances—'

'I haven't the least idea what you're talking about!'

'No, you haven't, have you? You never visited your father after he married someone called Kyle—my favourite aunt, as it happens. And we're a close family. Which makes you and me related by marriage. But *you* weren't allowed to visit, and you wouldn't even see your father after you grew up and had the choice. You didn't even come to his funeral last year, when you could have done. Well *I* liked your father very much, as it happens—'

'You would, you're obviously the same type!' Kate

spat the words instinctively. They were the only thing she could hold on to out of a whirling sense of bewilderment.

'Thank you. I take that as a compliment. As I said, I liked him very much. He was, though I can see you've been told the opposite, a thoroughly nice man!'

'Who deserted his wife and child.'

'Who got mixed up in a divorce situation which happens to a lot of people. I don't know the whole story behind it, and I don't suppose you do either. All right,' he said grimly, 'I'm not attacking your mother, that would hardly be fair. *I* only saw things from the other end. A happy, stable marriage after a lot of bitterness which everyone tried to forget about. You're very like him to look at,' he added, studying her. 'Like the photographs he used to keep of you, too. I often used to wonder what this stray cousin would be like if I ever met her. Later, after hearing the fact that she was obviously too neurotic to acknowledge her own father, I—'

'*That* really isn't any of your business! And,' Kate said between gritted teeth, 'I certainly wouldn't consider we were related in any way! So now, if you've finished digging up the past *quite* unnecessarily, would you please drive on?'

'Certainly,' he said grimly, and let in the clutch with such a jerk that she was thrown back in her seat. 'But you asked me, and I told you! I haven't told anyone else, so if Tessa wants to know why you're looking so shattered, you can tell her it's jet-lag. And, as I said, forget it! But if you were wondering why I hadn't exactly welcomed you with open arms, there's your reason. I could tell from the moment you turned round and looked at me so snootily at the airport what sort of person you'd grown up to be!'

Kate could only sit silently, fulminating. Such a comment didn't deserve an answer. Besides, she was too confused by the way the past had reared up suddenly to slap her in the face. It was too much, on top of travelling from one side of the world to the other. It would have been too much at any time. But what right had this man to comment on her family affairs—and on her character? And why shouldn't she have taken sides with the mother who had loved and looked after her?

Kate pushed aside the memory of the patience she had had to exert, since she grew up, with Mrs Raven's tendency to cling to the past, and to her only child. It was, after all, understandable. Just as understandable as her fastidiousness against getting married again, after being let down once.

The car turned sharply, rocking her against Nicholas Kyle, and before she could collect herself he was turning again, into a short, bumpy drive. Kate hadn't even noticed where they were in the shock of his direct attack, but she was suddenly aware that they were among a development of houses standing small and square and white, like sugar-lumps, each set in a small garden. And there, straightening up from a dusty, bright-orange Volkswagen Beetle, was the familiar figure of Tessa.

Nicholas Kyle gave a brief hoot on his horn as he drew up behind her, and leaned out of the window to call a greeting. Kate pulled a sharp rein on her temper. She had to, because Tessa was coming at once to tug her door open with a broad, beaming smile on her face. She looked just the same, if browner—small and boyish in jeans and a T-shirt, with close-cropped, light brown hair, freckles, big glasses. With her clever, plain little face, and the glasses, she had always looked like nothing so much as a very intelligent small boy.

'Katie, I'm sorry! I feel dreadful about not meeting you, but the car just wouldn't start!'

'Have you tried cleaning the plugs, like I told you?' Nicholas Kyle said cheerfully. His voice was so different from his tone of a few moments ago that Kate stared at him in disbelief. Tessa gave a rueful grin as she answered him.

'I did, but actually it was the battery. Somehow I'd let it go flat. David Rouse next door is charging it up for me. Yes, I know, a bit late! Oh, Katie, poor love, you look positively dazed. Thank goodness Nick was able to meet you! I didn't know what to do—'

'I could probably have taken a taxi,' Kate said, finding her voice and trying not to sound as if she would have preferred that alternative. If she was looking odd, she hoped her friend would put it down to the journey, but she carefully kept her eyes away from Nicholas Kyle as she got out of the car. It was with an effort that she put the cheerfulness which Tessa would be expecting from her into her voice as she added, 'I can't believe I'm really here at last!'

'I hope the car you're borrowing for your friend to get to work in is more reliable than yours,' Nicholas Kyle's voice said, 'or one of you is going to have to turn into an expert mechanic.' He came round the Holden and balanced lightly on the balls of his feet, looking down at Tessa. 'Want me to take a look at it, just for you?'

'No, it's still at the Townleys', and since he's a maintenance engineer it's bound to be all right, surely? We're going to pick it up this evening.' Tessa, who had several older brothers, seemed to take the offer for granted without noticing the 'just for you' which Kate was sure had been pointed, and in her direction.

At the same time she felt a sinking of her heart to see that Tessa was looking up at this man with open friendliness and none of her usual shyness—which, from Tessa, suggested she knew him well. And *he*, Kate thought with dislike, was turning on a charm which was probably automatic to him with most females. Then she had to pull herself together as Tessa turned to her again.

'Come on in, Katie. Oh dear, you do look white! They really are pushing it, wanting you to start work as soon as tomorrow, aren't they? It doesn't give you any time to get used to things! Nick, have you got time to come in for a coffee and be introduced to Kate properly?'

'No, I'd better get back to work. No doubt Kate and I will be seeing each other.' There was a dry note in his voice which Tessa didn't seem to notice. He had pulled Kate's cases out of the back of the station-wagon and set them carefully down at the side of the drive. Kate was determined not to thank him for the lift, but her silence seemed to go unremarked as he gave Tessa a cheerful grin which might have been supposed to include both of them, and climbed back into the driving seat. Kate hoped, devoutly, that she *wouldn't* see him again. Cousins-by-marriage indeed—and the type of man she most disliked!

Tessa was giving him a wave and calling out thanks as he backed out of the drive with rapid expertise. Kate deliberately didn't watch him, but turned to look at the house instead. It was small and boxy and gleamed white in the sun. A patch of marigolds glowed a bright orange next to the front door, surviving to bloom in the dry, dusty air. She was still feeling too dazed to notice much else when Tessa turned back to help her with her cases. They both went inside, to a coolness which was a sudden relief, but to a very ordinary interior with plain but practical furnishings. Tessa was chattering as they went.

'Oh, it is lovely to see you! I've been starved of company from home. And won't it be fun to be sharing again? I'm sorry all over again for not being able to meet you, but wasn't it lucky that Nick had to be at the airport to collect that package of special drugs? I knew he'd help out if he could, but he might have been in the middle of something. Still, it gave you the chance to meet him, and now there'll be someone you know at the hospital. In fact,' she said with a chuckle, 'it's quite a good way to meet your immediate boss.'

'He's *what*?'

'Didn't he tell you?' Tessa asked in surprise. 'Oh well, perhaps he didn't want to talk shop the minute you'd arrived. And I suppose I shouldn't call him that really. He's actually a general registrar, and they all do everything. But I know he spends a lot of time in obstetrics, so that they practically consider him attached. It fits in with the extra research he's doing into childhood infections related to poverty. He says it only makes sense to start from birth. But you're bound to see a lot of him, which will be nice, won't it, because he can help you settle in!'

Nice was so far from the word Kate would have chosen that she almost choked. She hadn't even realised that Nicholas Kyle was a doctor—though she supposed she should have done, from his remarks about the hospital—and it certainly hadn't occurred to her that she might be working with, or for, him. She was glad that Tessa was too busy leading her through the house to notice her shock. As they turned back to inspect the small kitchen she managed,

'Do you know him well?'

'Oh yes, we've known him ages. The Prof likes him too. We first met him in Somalia, when he was working with the Save The Children Fund there. Then, when we moved down here, we found he was already here, working at Mutala Hospital. It's like that on the expatriate circuit. You keep running into the same people.' Tessa turned round, and there was suddenly a tinge of pink in her cheeks—but before Kate could wonder what might have made her blush she was going on with swift sympathy, and with an expression of rueful amusement. 'Oh dear, poor Katie, I'm running on, and there's you looking all pale and shattered! You must be feeling the change in climate—you'd better sit down and put your feet up.'

'No, I'm—I'm all right. I expect I'm just suffering from jet-lag.' Kate even managed a laugh, though she didn't feel like one. That was the excuse Nicholas Kyle had told her to give, too, and although she was truthfully caught up in a sense of time-disorientation, she certainly didn't want to follow *his* advice. She said quickly, 'I'm fine. Honestly. I'm—I'm really glad to be here, too. Were you as surprised as you sounded when I wrote and said I was coming? You're not the only one with a sense of adventure, you know!'

That was the excuse she had given Tessa for coming. That, and the fact that she wanted to put her midwifery training to good use. It really had seemed like an adventure, too. Now, although she was careful not to let her light words show it, it was suddenly feeling less like an adventure than a disaster. She would be working for a man she had disliked on sight, and who had given her very good reasons for disliking him. A man who, furthermore, had condemned her even before she began.

But Richard Cranshaw was here, so she still ought to be glad she had come. Tessa, too, was a friend she had missed. And she was a good midwife, Kate thought stubbornly. She had always been considered particularly efficient, as Nicholas Kyle would find out, whether he wanted to admit it or not. She certainly wasn't going to let him put her off . . . .

CHAPTER TWO

SHE HAD her courage back by next morning, and drove on to the hospital site with a feeling of resolution.

Kate hadn't known what to expect of the hospital, but since she had been told that it had been officially opened only ten years ago, she had half expected a modern building of concrete and glass. Instead, she found herself driving into a low-level sprawl. It was made up of long, Nissen-type huts built on either side of covered walkways, and the only stone building was a one-storey square edifice in the middle.

She parked the car Tessa had borrowed for her from an expatriate family going on leave, and walked back to the administrative block, looking around her with interest. It was, she remembered, very much an African hospital *for* Africans, with its own Nurse Training School attached to train the Lanbwena staff. But it was hard not to feel daunted by the fact that she didn't see a single white face. Her own fairness seemed to stick out like the proverbial sore thumb, and made her feel strange. Glimpses through the Nissen hut windows were reassuring, however, because a hospital ward looked like a hospital ward anywhere. Notices saying 'Dispensary', 'Casualty' and 'Pathology' were familiar ground, too.

It had been a sharp disappointment to learn from Tessa that Richard Cranshaw wasn't based at the hospital at all, but at the university on the other side of town. There were better research facilities there. Tessa had mentioned, however, that the Professor came down to the hospital quite often, so Kate would just have to make the best of that . . .

She was to have a brief interview with Matron before starting work. Remembering, unwillingly, Nicholas Kyle's comments, Kate took care to look meek as the dark-skinned woman in her Matron's uniform looked her over coldly with an expression which suggested that, however well-qualified Miss Raven might be, she shouldn't expect preferential treatment. Kate assured Matron that she was quite happy to help train the Lanbwena nurses who must pass their midwifery exams before being considered qualified, and then she was free to go and draw her uniform from Stores. After she had changed she was to go straight to Maternity and report to the sister-in-charge.

The uniform was a plain white overall dress in thin cotton, with a tunic and trousers, also in white, for theatre work. Pinning on her State Registered Nurse and State Certified Midwife badges, and clipping a small white cap on to the smooth fairness of her hair, Kate felt a sense of relief at being back in uniform. It made her feel better, and stilled her uncertainties.

She came out on to the walkway to consult the small map she had been given, to see where to find Maternity. The hospital site seemed to stretch across a fair area of ground, and there were ten of the Nissen huts marked as wards, with the usual selection of surgical, medical and specialisations. Theatres were marked, and a large rectangle on the edge of the site seemed to be Out Patients. Kate had already passed that as she drove on to the site, she realised. There had been a long queue outside, even this early in the day. Now, which was the shortest way to Maternity?

'Starting work already, I see?'

Kate tried not to jump at the dry voice which sounded directly beside her, and felt a flash of annoyance as she looked up into Nicholas Kyle's grey eyes. He was recognisably a doctor now, in his white coat, but it made him look no less smoothly handsome and certainly no less arrogant, she decided. And he would have to come along when she was looking lost. His fairness, she thought involuntarily, made him stand out here as much as she did. If he had been anybody else she would have found it a relief. However, she had resolved overnight not to let his presence upset her, and if she *had* to work for him, the best she could do would be to treat him with a cool formality. She opened her mouth to answer, but he was going on.

'Scarcely giving you time to think, are they? I suppose you've had your interview with Matron? Didn't she put you off? She's a lady well known for not liking foreigners!' He seemed sardonically amused by Kate's instinctive glance round. 'Though "foreigners" doesn't only mean white ones. You'll find that to a true Lanbwena a foreigner is anyone not actually born here—and that includes your obstetric consultant, Mr Olinga, since he comes from Uganda. And Dr Achmed from Egypt, and even Dr Kani from Lesotho, which is practically next door. It can be confusing until you work out the system.'

'How did *you* get your job, then?' Kate asked. She hadn't meant to ask him, nor in that hostile tone, and swallowed in annoyance at the knowledge that she had already broken her resolution.

'Oh, I'm tolerated. As you will be, as long as you're prepared to be a useful pair of hands and do everything you're told to do without making a fuss about it. We're the only two white people here, by the way. Working in the hospital, I mean, on a permanent basis. So I hope that means you're going to behave yourself.'

'Certainly,' Kate said tightly. The sardonic look he was giving her wasn't helping her to keep cool. She bit her lip on her inclination to retort, and looked up at him formally. 'Since you know your way around here, Dr Kyle, perhaps you'd direct me to Maternity. I am supposed to be reporting there, not standing here talking.'

'I'll walk along with you, since I'm going that way.' He indicated, and then fell into step beside her. 'By the way, the hospital's got three-hundred-and-fifty beds and we're the only large medical centre for hundreds of miles. Apart from providing facilities for Mutala itself, we're the back-up for all the outlying clinics scattered around in the districts.'

'Thank you, but I was told the details of the hospital before I came out here.'

'Already thinking you know it all? And there was I, thinking I was being helpful. Just in case you were expecting the place to be run exactly like your teaching hospital!'

'I wasn't expecting that, and I don't—' Kate bit her lip again. He really was determined to put her in the wrong. He might not think she'd cope with working here, but she would. Apart from the climate, to which no doubt she'd get used, she couldn't see any reason why she shouldn't. 'I gather you're the—the obstetric registrar?' she said carefully, trying to sound dignified, and willing to be informed.

'No. I have registrar status, but I'm attached to several things. It's like that here.' He glanced down at her, giving her a faintly mocking look. 'You do expect things to be run just like London, don't you?'

'No, I don't! I wouldn't have the sense I was born with if I thought—' Kate broke off. 'I was merely asking a polite question,' she said, trying not to sound as if she was gritting her teeth.

'Then I'll answer it politely. There's a shortage of doctors, and always will be, I suppose, until they can start producing them from the medical school they've just started up at the university.' He paused to nod at someone passing and murmured something which sounded like, 'Dr Jericho,' by way of explanation to Kate.

She was aware that she had received a look of faint curiosity from the other doctor, and wondered with a brief feeling of uncertainty how long it would take her to be able to learn everyone's name and status.

Nicholas Kyle was going on. 'It means we all do everything, no matter what our standing. So I might find myself taking out an appendix one minute, diagnosing a cancer the next, then looking at a bilharzia, then seeing to the usual crop of children with gastro-enteritis or bronchitis. It all adds to the interest. Oh, and then there are the road traffic accidents. You wouldn't think you'd get many of those in a country with as much space as Lanbwe, but you do. People are always driving too fast and smashing themselves up. Then there are the eye cases, of course. This is cattle country, so you get a lot of eye diseases.'

'Do the nursing staff move around too?'

'Only in training. Don't worry, if you're a midwife you'll stay a midwife. And be kept busy enough, too!'

Kate hadn't been worrying, she had merely been interested. Particularly interested to hear what kind of cases Mutala Hospital handled, which sounded reasonably similar to those in any other hospital if you added in the tropical infections. From anybody else, too, she would have thought the mini-lecture was designed to be helpful.

She glanced up at him, to find him watching her, and felt immediately defensive. Why on earth did he and she have to be the only two white people working in the hospital? She had felt a jerk of uneasiness, and some annoyance, to hear him say that it was so. There had been several white faces to be seen in the brief tour round Mutala Tessa had given her last night. And all their Dendaa neighbours seemed to be white, too. But here, the only person with whom she had an automatic link was Nicholas Kyle . . .

'We're here,' he said coolly, making her realise that

they had drawn to a halt a moment ago. His expression suggested that he was aware of what she had been thinking, and was mockingly amused by it. 'I won't come in and introduce you to Myrtle—Sister Labatsu to you. You'll have to learn to stand on your own feet, won't you? Besides, it won't do you any harm to be thrown in at the deep end, and I've got a clinic to run. Goodbye for now, Kate. No doubt I'll see you around!'

It would have been childish to retort, *Not if I see you first*, and Kate was angry with herself for having to bite it back. It would have been a highly unsuitable comment, anyway, to a doctor for whom she would apparently have to work. She had just been thinking, though, that the one advantage of his being the only white doctor here would be that, outside the ward, she would always be able to see him coming—and dodge!

He was walking away from her now, with his casual easy stride, and she firmly resisted the temptation to watch him out of sight, or to feel faintly lost because he had gone. *That* was an idiotic thought, when he was the last person she wanted to have to see. She turned on her heel quickly and surveyed the Nissen hut outside which she was standing. She was here: she had better go in.

It really was a question of plunging in at the deep end, she found a few moments later. Sister Labatsu didn't eye her coldly as Matron had done, and as Nicholas Kyle's comments had made her half expect, but she was plainly having a busy morning. She greeted Kate with an abstracted air of relief, said, 'Ah good, I've been expecting you,' and immediately sent her to deliver a baby before she'd even shown her round.

It was a straightforward birth. Kate had just happened to arrive when four mothers were in the final

stages of labour all at the same time, in the sectioned-
off central area of the hut which formed the unit's
delivery room. She didn't even have time to do more
than notice that the trainee who was sent to assist
her seemed an efficient nurse and, thankfully, spoke
English, switching between languages quite easily.
Kate had been told that all the teaching in the hospital
was done in English but it was a relief to find that
the accent didn't give her any problems. And it was
useful to have a translator, too, since the mother only
spoke her own native dialect.

Wrapping the small, damp bundle of humanity in a
dressing-towel after checking, weighing and labelling
this new scrap of life, Kate looked down at the crumpled
dark brown face with a sudden sense of wonder—and
then with an involuntary grin as the little mouth suddenly gaped open in a yawn.

Her first African baby! And she'd been here how
long? Less than an hour? Well, it hadn't been so
different from delivering a baby anywhere else, and
this was the bit she always liked best about Maternity
work; the miracle of a new, healthy baby, which never
seemed any less of a marvel however many times it
happened.

With the first flap over, she was able to take stock of
her surroundings as she went back to report to Sister
Labatsu. In the main ward, beds lined the walls in neat
rows. Here, there was a drip up; there, a mother turned
restlessly in the first stage of labour. It was a friendly,
familiar scene.

The nurses all wore the same white uniforms but
some had a coloured chevron on one shoulder. Kate
was surprised to see two males amongst the nurses,
since there wasn't a large number of male midwives in
England. She remembered, then, being told that the
Lanbwena nurses weren't considered registered without
midwifery and that everyone had to do it. Perhaps that

explained the fact that the ward seemed to be quite
well-staffed, even though there seemed to be very few
nurses with the navy blue belt Kate wore to show that
she was a staff midwife. Only Sister wore a blue uniform,
and a frilly cap, which made her stand out as being the
person in authority.

'Well now, Staff Nurse, perhaps I've got time to give
you a quick tour,' Sister Labatsu announced a few
moments later. She gave a swift glance round before
sweeping Kate off in her wake.

'The Unit's divided into three sections, as you can
see—Admissions and First Stage down this end, and a
few beds for people with complications; then Second
Stage and Delivery Room; then a Post-Natal section at
the far end here. Sluice and instrument cupboards—no,
Nurse,' she broke off to instruct a trainee who had
looked round at their arrival, 'you'll just have to wipe
those down with neat Savlon, the second steriliser isn't
working again. Goodness knows I've rung the maintenance department enough times this week! These are the
delivery packs, Staff Nurse Raven. We use a great many
of those, as you may imagine. I wish I could say we
always had some in hand, but apart from the few we
always keep for emergencies, I'm afraid we don't. Now,
here we have the premature babies' room.'

The Prem Room was so basic, as Sister opened the
door to show it to her, that Kate kept her face carefully
blank. It was nothing but a tiny room with three incubators, two cribs and a table. An even smaller room next
to it held nothing but four upright chairs and was,
apparently, where the mothers of the premature babies
came to feed them. Since no one was feeding at the
moment Sister closed the door again and paused to
introduce Kate to a staff nurse who was attending to a
tiny, frail-looking babe in one of the incubators. The
staff nurse was called Rose Angkina, and gave Kate a
friendly look above her mask. No one so far had *seemed*

to resent her presence. Kate pulled herself quickly out
of a tendency to dwell on Nicholas Kyle's deliberate
discouragement, since Sister was talking to her as she
led her back through the Unit again.

'And that's all, except for Ante-Natal, which I'll show
you later. Let me see now, what haven't I told you? We
keep our mothers and babies in for forty-eight hours,
as routine. Most of them live miles away in the villages,
but with the nearer ones we still make follow-up visits
after ten days to see how the baby's progressing. The
trainees go out on those. I'll try to send you on one
when we can spare you, but I try to keep my trained
midwives for deliveries. You'll have done theatre work,
I suppose?'

'Yes, Sister.'

'Good, because we have to send someone in from
Maternity when there's a Caesarean. And unless we're
lucky enough to get Dr Kyle—or Dr Kani, she's had
quite a lot of experience too—my midwives know more
about birth than the surgeons do!'

Kate kept her face expressionless, though as a comment it wasn't promising. Perhaps it was just a ward
sister's scorn for the medical staff. She hoped so. She
hoped, too, that Sister hadn't noticed her slight jump
at Nicholas Kyle's name.

'When do the doctors make ward rounds, Sister?' she
asked.

'They don't,' Sister said promptly. 'We're lucky
enough if we see Mr Olinga for more than one Ante-
Natal clinic a month. *I* take them the rest of the time.
Well, it's hardly the man's fault. He's in charge of the
gynaecology department too, which gives him a long list
of operations. Most of the time, when we need a doctor,
we just have to phone round for one.' She glanced at
Kate and added, 'Luckily for us, Dr Kyle comes in when
he can. Perhaps you know him, since he's a compatriot
of yours?'

'I have met him, Sister. I don't know him at all well,' Kate added stiffly, aware that Sister was giving her a curious glance.

'No? I wondered if you might have trained at the same place or something. It's unusual for people to apply for jobs here. They usually find South Africa more glamorous, or prefer one of the East African countries where the climate's better. If you knew someone here it might have helped you to feel more settled. I'm sure you'll find Dr Kyle very helpful, anyway.' Luckily she dismissed the subject with that.

'I must show you the duty roster and work out your hours. Can you work until four this afternoon? That shift usually starts at seven-thirty a.m., but since you arrived mid-morning and it's your first day, I won't ask you to do second shift and stay on until seven.'

The trainee Kate had been working with on the delivery had been called Ethel. Looking at the duty roster, Kate discovered that all the trainees had similarly Victorian first-names. They were addressed by them, too, which was a relief considering that, to Kate's unfamiliar eye, their surnames all looked unpronounceable. The two young men were called Jacob and Isaac.

Sister gave Kate her duty-hours, and then said, 'Perhaps you'd like to spend some time familiarising yourself with all the different parts of the Unit today, so that you can find out where everything is for yourself. Then tomorrow you'll be able to be left in charge if necessary. I shall be off duty, and if my other staff nurse has to go on call-out, someone has to be in charge of the place. We've got some good trainees, but they aren't supposed to take full responsibility until they're finally qualified.'

'Are there many call-outs, Sister?' Kate asked, trying not to feel a nervous sinking in her stomach at the thought of being left in charge so soon. She hadn't quite

realised that there would be so few fully-trained staff.
But of course, she told herself quickly, she *would* manage, and it was a kind of compliment to find that Sister
must obviously think so.

'Oh, they happen every so often. We cover such a
large radius, and some of the mothers *will* leave it too
late to come in. Then, of course, we have to go out to
them. I've delivered babies just about everywhere, in
my time,' Sister said cheerfully. Then she was called
away down the ward, and Kate was left to pull herself
together and remind herself that, with all her training,
there was no reason why she shouldn't find this job as
easy as any other. No matter who tried to make her feel
that she wouldn't.

She worked through until four, reminding herself
every time she looked for something the Unit didn't
possess that she was in a strange country now, and not
in a large London teaching hospital. It was hard not
to remember Nicholas Kyle's comments as she found
herself automatically critical of a shortage of equipment
which sometimes seemed horrifying, and of a lack of
facilities which everybody else seemed to take for
granted. The frail baby in the Prem Room, for instance,
might have been on a heart-monitor—except that there
wasn't one. And the broken steriliser was one of only
two which seemed to be all the sterilising equipment
the Unit had. The delivery packs were parcelled up and
sent to be autoclaved in another part of the hospital.
That was somewhere else she would have to learn how
to find . . .

'I'm bushed,' she told Tessa ruefully some hours later,
when her friend came back to the house to find Kate
simply sitting there, wrapped in her light cotton
dressing-gown with her feet up. 'I seem to have spent
all day simply trying to find my way around.' Then with
a sudden wariness which came with the memory that
Tessa might relay any comments she might make, she

added quickly, 'I thoroughly enjoyed it, though. It's going to be a very interesting job!'

'I'm glad. Poor Katie, though, you do look tired!'

'It's just that my body doesn't seem to know what time it is.' Jet-lag really did seem to have caught up with her, making her feel blurred. 'And just when I manage to sort it out, I'll probably get sent on night duty, too! I gather we have to alternate, instead of doing a few months of each at a time!' She pulled a rueful face at her friend, and added, 'I think I would have gone to bed already if I could have found the energy to get there. Sorry not to be more sociable.'

'It's all right, I've got to work this evening anyway. I only came back to see how you'd got on.' Tessa gave her a sympathetic look. 'Yes, you *had* better catch up on some sleep, hadn't you? Did you see anything of Nick?'

'We ran into one another.' Apart from that first meeting, she'd seen him in the canteen during lunch and had avoided him, deliberately. Lunch had seemed remarkably heavy for this hot climate too, consisting of beef stew or steak, when Kate was yearning for a cold salad. She already knew that literally all foodstuffs had to be imported into Lanbwe, apart from the staple beef from its cattle-herds, because it was too much of a drought country to grow its own food. But she had missed the greenstuff and fruit which made up her usual diet. It had made her realise, though, why Richard Cranshaw might choose to settle here to continue his research into kwashiorkor, the malnutrition disease endemic to Africa. The memory of him made her glance up at Tessa now with a pretence of lightness.

'Do you often have to work in the evenings? I was hoping I might see the Prof sometime. Just to renew the acquaintance and ask him how the work's going! I mean,' she added, trying to sound casual rather than defensive, 'it'd only be polite, wouldn't it?'

'I've told him you're here. He does remember you.
Well, you know how vague he is. He *says* he does.'
Tessa gave Kate one of her exasperated looks, though
she had flushed a little, almost as if she felt responsible
for her employer's bad memory. 'We're a bit busy at
the moment because he's been co-opted to give some
lectures in the new medical school. Besides, the other
pathologist who was working with us went back to
America last month. Oh, when you saw Nick, did he
say—'

'We barely spoke. It's very busy there, you know.' If
Tessa was going to bring Nicholas Kyle's name into
every conversation, Kate decided, it really was going to
set her teeth on edge. She went on quickly, 'We had
half a patient's family camping outside this afternoon
after they'd brought her in, and I'm told they often do
that—lighting fires in the car park to cook over, too, if
someone doesn't go out and ask them not to! They all
got a ride in on a lorry, including the heavily-pregnant
mum. It's lucky she didn't start delivering en route!
Sorry,' she glanced up at Tessa with a grin which had a
touch of defiance in it. 'You're used to all that, aren't
you? And I didn't expect them to arrive in a red London
bus, honestly!'

'Rather less than you expected Mutala's main shopping street to be called The Mall, or that the Parlia-
ment buildings would be imitation Gothic,' Tessa said
with a chuckle. 'It *is* a purpose-built capital, that's
why it looks so . . . well, transplanted! What did you
make of the hospital, though? Will you like it, do
you think?'

'Well, it's different. But why shouldn't I like it?' Kate
pushed away her doubts and the confusion she'd been
feeling all day, and her voice came out almost on a
snap. 'Why does everyone seem to think I'll find it so
difficult? Just because I'm used to working in London
doesn't mean that I can't—'

'Oh no, I didn't mean that! It's just that everyone has difficulties in adjusting to Africa when they first come out. It—it kind of changes you.' Tessa looked thoughtful, and then broke out in a grin. 'You should get Nick to tell you about the Lanbwe social structure some time. He's learnt quite a lot of the language, too, as well as the Swahili he already knows. And he's only been here about six months.'

'Really? He gave me the impression he knew *all* about Africa.' Kate wasn't quite able to keep the cold note out of her voice this time, but before she could go on with something to distract Tessa's attention, she found that her friend was looking at her with too much curiosity. And some dismay.

'Oh dear, you haven't taken against Nick, have you? I hope not, because I sent him a message inviting him in for a meal some time. Oh, how awkward! He really is a particular friend of mine—'

Her guilty look suddenly suggested *how* particular a friend, and made Kate's heart sink. She wouldn't have thought the plain, shy Tessa was Nicholas Kyle's type at all—however much he might turn on the charm towards her just because she was there. Somehow she found herself feeling angry, purely on Tessa's behalf, because it seemed all wrong for her to be fascinated by such a smooth-talking type. On the other hand, she supposed it was Tessa's business.

'I don't like him much,' she said quickly, 'but that doesn't mean that you can't. He just isn't the sort of person I go for.'

'But he's really nice! And I can't think why. Oh well, I can't imagine what he can have done to upset you, but I'll tell him off when I see him!'

'No, don't. I just think he's—he's the flashy type, that's all. But if you like him, that's your affair!' Kate found she was glaring and knew she could have handled it better,

but she really was too tired to cope with the added problem of her feelings about Nicholas Kyle. 'When I first
saw him,' she found herself snapping, 'he was chatting up
the airline stewardess. In fact I thought he must be her
boyfriend, from the way they were carrying on. But if
he's a friend of yours, and you really like that sort of
person, I suppose I shouldn't say—'

'Oh Kate, you really do sound prim! I thought you'd
have grown out of being like that by now!'

'Well, thanks!'

'Sorry,' Tessa said mollifyingly in the face of Kate's
angry surprise. 'For goodness' sake let's not quarrel!
Look, have you had something to eat, or shall I make
you something? That's what I came back here for,
really, to make us both some supper and to see how
your first day went. But you're quite wrong about
Nick, anyway. He—he can't help being handsome,
and he's actually one of the kindest and most reliable
people I know! Let alone that he's a thoroughly good
doctor, and that ought to count for something with
you, surely!'

She had swept round and out into the kitchen without
giving Kate a chance to answer—which was just as well,
because they obviously weren't going to agree on the
subject of Nicholas Kyle. Kate felt hurt, too, by Tessa's
criticism. Had her friend always thought . . .? It almost
sounded as if Tessa's opinion of her was the same as Dr
Kyle's, and it was much worse to hear it from *her*, when
she didn't have any axe to grind. But Tessa was her
friend . . .

Tessa's voice called out to say that it was eggs or eggs
because that seemed to be all they'd got in the fridge,
and Kate found herself answering her normally. There
was really no reason for her to suddenly feel weepy
over a minor disagreement. She pulled herself together
quickly, telling herself that it was ridiculous if travelling

and a change of climate could have that much effect on her. That, obviously, was all it was.

When Tessa left, after seeing that Kate was fed and telling her in a motherly fashion to go to bed and sleep off the time-change, nothing more had been said about their sudden spat. In fact they had even managed to laugh together, almost normally, about Kate's air of being about to drop off to sleep in the middle of eating an omelette.

She was on duty again at seven-thirty the following morning so she crawled into bed feeling that the alarm would ring all too soon. She wasn't going to think about Tessa's earnest defence of Dr Nicholas Kyle, nor the way she had flushed and looked oddly sparkly as she talked about him. If Tessa was in love, that was *her* business. Kate certainly didn't have to feel aggrieved because Nick had disliked her so much before they had even met. Her lip curled as she remembered Tessa saying that he couldn't help being so handsome— though, to be fair, perhaps he couldn't. But he was also odious and overbearing and, somehow, far too magnetic to be ignored.

Kate turned her mind quickly to Richard Cranshaw with a feeling of relief, even if there was also a touch of defiance in it. Well, there was no reason why she shouldn't wonder when she would see him.

She slept at last and tossed her way through jumbled dreams. Waking abruptly to the brightness of morning, she was aware that they had been of a yellow, dusty landscape, and a wide, wide sky which seemed to go on for ever. And, annoyingly, Nicholas Kyle had walked through her dream with her, mocking her, always just ahead of whatever she was doing and so irritatingly knowledgeable that she was made to feel stupid and inadequate.

Vividly, in the moment of waking, she was sure that at some time in the dream he had held out a

branch of a Lanbwena thorn tree to her and taunted
her that she didn't dare catch hold of it for fear of
pricking herself, It was such a stupid image that she
shook it off and got up feeling bad-tempered. Surely
she wasn't going to be haunted by the man asleep as
well as awake, was she?

She went on duty still tired, and was relieved when
the senior staff nurse, Rose Angkina, didn't get called
away from the ward and leave her to run things. It
was a day without crises, and Kate began to feel a
little more at home in the Nissen hut with its rows
of beds, and among the patients who didn't seem to
mind that she had to communicate with them by signs
unless another nurse was with her to act as interpreter.

At least the treatments were the same, she thought
as she donned a stethoscope to listen to the flutter of a
foetal heart and palpated the distended stomach of a
new admission to check whether labour had genuinely
started or not. The post-natal babies were the same too,
with their croaky cries for attention and their need to
be changed and weighed and handed to the mothers for
feeding and then weighed again. The little prem seemed
to be flourishing, in spite of the lack of sophisticated
equipment. He was lucky to be the only one at the
moment, Rose Angkina told Kate with casual cheerfulness, because there were usually several. And when
there were more than three they had to double them
up in the incubators, which could be a risk if there was
any likelihood of infection.

Kate was glad that Nicholas Kyle didn't come into
the Unit to make her feel self-conscious, and when
they did have to call in a doctor to a mother who
was showing signs of a chest infection, it was Dr Kani
who came—a black lady doctor whose accent was
different from the Lanbwena lilt. She arrived in
theatre-clothes, stayed briefly to write up an antibiotic,
and went away again to act as anaesthetist for a

theatre list. Apparently that was the way of it for the medical staff, who were used, Kate remembered, to doing absolutely everything . . .

She came off duty in the afternoon feeling that the hospital was beginning to sort itself out in her mind, seeming less like an anonymous sprawl than a place she was beginning to know. As she came out to walk across the car park, into the dry heat which felt like an unusually good summer but which was, she knew, Lanbwe's autumn, Kate felt the gritty wind which never seemed to stop blowing in the day-time, and wriggled a little at the sandy feeling it gave her skin. It hadn't, though, been as tiring a day as it was yesterday, so perhaps she was already getting acclimatised. She walked towards the car—and then, suddenly, on a converging course, she saw a familiar tall, thin figure.

She hadn't expected to see Richard Cranshaw here, at this moment, and for a second she felt completely nonplussed. A fit of shyness made her feel almost inclined to walk on. He hadn't noticed her, because he was walking along in his usual abstraction. And would he recognise her? She was watching him with her heart in her eyes, when somebody suddenly called his name from directly beside her. Turning sharply, with a feeling of disbelief she saw Nicholas Kyle climbing out of a nearby car; and at the same moment the Professor came right up to her with his eyes switching from vagueness to a sudden surprised recognition.

'Why, it's Nurse Raven, isn't it? Kate, Tessa's friend? Yes, of course it is! I'm sorry, I was miles away. Hold on a moment, Nick, I seem to have run into an old friend!'

The last person she would have wanted to witness her running into Professor Cranshaw was Nicholas Kyle. Why on earth did he have to be just here, just now?

Kate was all too aware of the fact that he was standing there, watching.

'Hallo, Professor Cranshaw,' she said formally. And then, because he was still looking faintly puzzled, she added quickly, 'I've come to work out here. Tessa did say she'd told you.'

'Yes, she did. I hadn't really forgotten.' He was giving her the sweet, deprecating smile which had always made her heart turn over and which lit the eyes as blue as her own with a rueful humour. 'Tessa's always telling me off for being absent-minded, but I promise you, I hadn't really forgotten you. Considering the extra interest you always took in pathology, I wouldn't be likely to, would I? Kate,' he said pleasantly, turning to Nicholas Kyle, 'was one of my better students among the nursing staff—though, of course, she may have listened to my lectures so intently out of politeness, because she shared a flat with my assistant! Oh, do you two know each other?'

'Yes, we've met. Sorry to break up a meeting between old friends, Richard, but if I'm going to give you a lift to this meeting—'

'Yes, of course, but we've got time, haven't we? They can't start without us. How nice it is to see you again, Kate. I'm sure you're going to be a very valuable addition to the nursing staff here. Don't you think so, Nick?'

'If *you* think so, I'm sure that's a point in her favour,' Nicholas Kyle said with the merest touch of a drawl, making Kate feel, angrily, that he wasn't prepared to give an inch. The Professor didn't seem to notice it, however, because he was still giving her his full attention with the politeness which had always characterised him.

'What made you decide to come out here? I'm sure you must have had excellent career prospects in

England. And you haven't got married and vanished into domesticity like so many of the nurses?'

'No, I . . .' Kate wished Nicholas Kyle didn't have to be standing by, listening and watching and making her feel tongue-tied with annoyance. Her heart might have been singing at the friendly and interested look Richard Cranshaw was giving her if it hadn't been for that. 'Tessa and I have been writing to each other ever since you—you left,' she said, swallowing hard to make sure she wasn't blushing, 'and it all sounded so interesting—'

'That you decided to try Africa too? What an excellent idea. And how nice for her to have your company too. She's probably been homesick.' He looked a little surprised at the thought and added absently, 'I think I work her too hard. Ought I to give her more time off, I wonder?'

'I'm sure she doesn't mind, Professor Cranshaw.'

'Richard. We don't have to be formal out here, do we? Yes, Nick, I *am* coming,' he said abruptly, almost as if he was aware of a feeling of impatience from his colleague, who stood silently by. Almost as if, too, he was regretting it, Kate thought with a sudden lift of the heart and a sparkling sense of wonder as Richard Cranshaw gave her his sweet smile again. 'You must come up to the university some time,' he said pleasantly. 'But in any case, I'm sure we'll be seeing you!'

'That would be nice.'

'And quite unavoidable in a community this size,' Nicholas Kyle said softly, and on a hard note, so that only Kate could hear it as the Professor turned away to get in the car. She felt the shock of the tall, fair doctor's open dislike for a brief moment before he too turned away. It had been quite deliberate.

He really was the most atrociously rude man she had ever met. But then, he had been determined to hate her even before he met her. She wasn't going to let that spoil the pleasure of the last few moments, was she?

No, she certainly wasn't. Not with Richard Cranshaw's immediate friendliness to remember, and the sheer pleasure of seeing him again. In fact there was no need to waste any thoughts at all on a man who was so much the Professor's opposite in both looks and manner that he might have been a different species. And Kate certainly knew which species she preferred—there was no contest!

She should be feeling a glow about seeing the Professor again, instead of brooding about Nicholas Kyle. Quelling her discomfort, Kate put him determinedly out of her head. The best thing she could do about *him* was to keep out of his way as far as possible.

CHAPTER THREE

IT WASN'T exactly easy to keep out of his way when he turned up in Maternity the next morning to see a patient who was showing dangerous signs of eclampsia. They had put out a call for a doctor, and it was Dr Kyle's fair head which came round the screens.

Watching his unhurried carefulness with the patient, Kate had to admit, grudgingly, that he was a good doctor. His manner with the woman was gentle and reassuring and he teased her gently in her own language. Kate watched him with unwilling admiration and was somehow glad when Sister Labatsu took her place and sent her to help a trainee who was worried whether a delivery was imminent or not. Although Nicholas Kyle had treated her presence with nothing more than an impersonal formality, Kate still found it oddly disturbing to have to stand beside him—let alone the fact that she was sure he was waiting for her to make some mistake.

It was unfortunate that she was just struggling with a tight valve on an oxygen cylinder when he re-emerged from behind the screens. Before she knew he was even there, a hand came over her shoulder and turned the firmly stuck wheel with an easy flick of the wrist. She looked up defensively and saw the grey eyes watching her with a cold, sardonic gaze which was quite different from his gentleness a few moments ago with the patient.

'You were probably turning it the wrong way. When in doubt, read the instructions. But of course, you have a stubborn streak, don't you?'

He had turned on his heel and was walking away before she could retort. A few moments later, she found Sister Labatsu was calling for her down the ward.

43

'Staff Nurse, I'm going to leave you in charge of the elampsia patient while I go on call-out. I'd send you, but I don't think you'd better go on your first outside delivery until I can find someone experienced to go with you, so I'll have to go myself. Oh, and by the way, Dr Kyle reminded me that you shouldn't go on night duty until you're properly settled in, so remind me to change that duty roster so that you won't have to do nights for the first three weeks, will you?'

'I'm sure I could manage, Sister.'

'No, he's quite right. It's not fair to give you irregular hours too soon after travelling. Now then, if our possible elampsia gets any worse, see if you can get Dr Kyle back at once, will you? One of the other doctors if he's not available, but try asking particularly for him.'

For a moment Kate wondered bitterly whether Dr Kyle had also advised Sister not to trust her new staff nurse with an outside delivery. She could scarcely argue with Sister's ruling, anyway; and as sense reasserted itself she knew that Sister could have decided for herself that Kate was still not experienced enough to do a village delivery on her own.

All the same, as Sister collected up the equipment to take out to the ambulance and told a junior trainee to accompany her, Kate felt broody behind the calm expression she put on for Sister's benefit. Well, at least she was trusted enough to be put in charge here, and if she had to send for a doctor, she hoped it wouldn't be Dr Kyle who turned up. She supposed she ought to be grateful to him for the advice about night duty, even though she was sure he'd suggested it out of distrust, rather than concern for her welfare!

When he did come back to the ward there wasn't time for gratitude, unwilling or otherwise, because there was a rush for an emergency Caesarean. Kate had to send the most senior trainee into theatre for it once Nicholas Kyle had given the instructions, and she was sure he was critical about that. However, a new prem was giving problems and Kate certainly wasn't prepared to leave that to someone untrained.

In fact, she was feeling slightly panicky about the lack of medical staff to call for advice, though she certainly didn't show it as she gave orders to the trainees and kept her usual calm expression in place. She kept it in place, too, as she reported to Sister Labatsu on her eventual return, able to say that the new baby's breathing problems had been safely resolved; that the eclampsia patient had had a successful Caesarean but was now poorly; and that there had been three new births and one admission. Since Sister seemed to feel that she had managed very well, it was a pity that Dr Kyle wasn't still in the ward to hear her say so.

Kate was too busy concentrating on settling in over the next few days, to think about anything else at all—even to wonder when she might run into Richard again. She had mentioned to Tessa, lightly, that she had met him, but since the small house provided the two girls with a bedroom each and they worked very different hours, they were more likely to see each other in passing than meet for long.

Tessa had, however, taken care to start introducing Kate to their neighbours, all of whom treated her with immediate friendliness. Dendaa seemed to be almost entirely populated by married couples, many of them with children, but there was an easy friendship among the expatriate community and Kate was told by several people to drop by any time she was free. There were invitations, too, to join in family picnics when she had a free day. The invitations were extended to Tessa too, of course, and 'that boss of yours, if you can ever drag him away from his lab!'—a comment which made Kate prick up her ears hopefully.

However, at the moment her working hours were long enough to make her feel disinclined to be sociable when she was off duty. She slept and worked, and wished the one non-black face in the hospital didn't always turn up when she was having difficulties—mistaking the route to the dispensary, or unable to find the right form to fill out to say a mother should be checked for tuberculosis, or hunting in the wrong place for the right size of tubing to suck out the mucus from a premature baby's throat.

It was bad enough to see that recognisable fair head appearing round the door of the unit with monotonous regularity, and finding that while he treated Kate with impersonal formality or quiet sarcasm, he was pleasant enough to everyone else to be a general favourite . . .

He wasn't in evidence when Sister decided, at last, to send Kate on her first call-out. Like any other maternity department, the Unit seemed to alternate between rushes and periods of quiet—when, in some hospitals but not this one, inductions would have been started to even things out. It was a temporary quiet spell when the emergency call came in, so Sister felt she could part with two staff nurses at once. Rose Angkina was delegated to go with Kate to show her the drill. Kate was glad about that, since she had found Rose pleasant and friendly.

The two girls gathered up the equipment and hurried across to the ambulance park where a driver was standing leaning against the vehicle waiting for them. They would bring the patient back with them, because that was routine after even safe deliveries, so that the mother and baby could spend the usual two days in hospital being given post-natal care.

'Put the bag and the delivery pack in the back,' Rose instructed, 'and we'll go up in front with the driver for the moment.' She gave Kate a grin, adding, 'Nice to be out of the ward, isn't it? Though let's just hope the ambulance doesn't break down!'

'Heavens, do they often?'

'Not as much as all that. But if they do, we're the ones who have to go for help—the drivers aren't allowed to leave the vehicles. If they do, every spare part gets stripped off before they can get back. It's really amazing what people will steal,' Rose said with a sniff, 'though they don't look on it that way!'

Kate climbed into the front without comment and the driver started the engine. He was uniformed, with a black peaked cap, dark trousers and a white short-sleeved shirt, though Kate had gathered that the ambulance drivers were simply drivers and didn't have any medical experience. Rose gave him brief instructions as to the route and they began at once to pull out of the hospital site.

'Are we going far?' Kate asked above the engine noise.

'It's about seventy miles,' Rose said casually. The distance didn't seem to mean much to her. It might not, Kate supposed wonderingly, in such a large and mainly empty country.

'How did we get the message?'

'Oh, someone on a bicycle will have gone to the nearest main road and found a bar or a garage with a telephone. We'll find him waiting for us at the turn-off, to show us the rest of the way.'

It sounded practical, if primitive. Kate crushed memories of a telephone box to every half a mile and a doctor or hospital to every town, and reminded herself that she was in Africa now. She could hardly forget it as they passed through the outer suburbs of Mutala at speed and broke abruptly into open country. Here, she saw with a touch of surprise, there was some cultivation instead of the usual scrub, and a tractor was chugging its way to and fro across dusty ridges of turned earth. It must be one of the government schemes, aimed to grow at least something in the arid earth—even though the crops were never enough.

Cultivation dropped behind them and the asphalt road went on alone through the inevitable dry scrub. The country's flatness gave the feeling of seeing for miles, vision only impeded by the dusty haze in the air. Kate realised how little she had seen of Lanbwe so far in her simple journeying from Dendaa to the hospital and back, and felt a stir of excitement to be moving away from Mutala.

In the distance she caught sight of a small boy in shorts, waving a stick at a handful of cattle. It was the first time she had seen any of Lanbwe's staple beef, and they looked skinny and long-horned.

The ambulance driver was taking them along at a steady speed, though with an easy lean on the steering wheel which suggested carelessness, and Kate found herself with a brief, uneasy memory of Nicholas Kyle's comments on Lanbwena driving. The ambulancemen, though, must surely be employed for their carefulness? Certainly there didn't seem to be anything reckless in the way he passed a Land Rover going the other way, and then a bullock-cart moving slowly along in their own direction. There seemed to be very few people about in all this emptiness, so that it was like skimming through a hot, deserted landscape.

Another scattering of cattle appeared, moving slowly amongst the thorn trees, with another small boy tending them. They passed a petrol-tanker, looking surprisingly urban out here, and then a garage standing all alone beside the road with a café attached to it. Then, abruptly, Kate was jerked to attention and found herself saying involuntarily, 'Oh, look . . .'

In single file along the side of the road ahead there were natives—*real* natives, Kate thought with fascination—walking in an odd procession of suddenly bright, exotic clothes, scarlets and blues mixed up together and a bright primrose-yellow and a glitter of beads.

These people were covered from head to toe in layers of their vivid robes and wore elaborate head-dresses made of high turbans of folded material. They carried yokes across their shoulders with what looked like metal pots and pans hanging from them, and walked with a slow stateliness which seemed to ignore the world around them. The faces she caught as they passed were very dark and almost aquiline, quite unlike the Lanbwena Kate had seen so far. She craned out of the open window to look at them as they passed—and then felt awkwardly that Rose must think she was behaving like a tourist, gazing at her countrymen like that. Rose, however, said,

'You haven't see the Herero before? They only turn up now and again. They must be going into town. I expect they'll camp by the railway station. The Herero are nomads. They go all over the whole of Africa—and they don't keep to any laws except their own,' she added in a tone of disapproval.

'They're very colourful,' Kate said meekly. It was fairly plain that the Lanbwena didn't approve too much of the Herero.

'Yes, I suppose so. They don't believe in schools or hospitals, so I'm told. It must be difficult to change, if you come from that kind of tribe,' Rose said dismissively. The driver said something then, in Lanbwena, and chuckled, and Rose gave him an answering smile. They all lapsed into silence again as they sped on.

Rose obviously couldn't see anything to admire in the Herero way of life, Kate decided, and no doubt she was right, though Kate herself had felt a stir of the imagination at the almost kingly way the nomads had walked with their heads held high and their vivid costumes catching the sun. There was a freedom about them which took her back suddenly to childhood story-books and roused long-ago dreams.

They seemed, to her, like a glimpse of real Africa.

Not that it wasn't all real. She realised suddenly that the sheer sense of space, the dry heat, even the rush and make-do of Mutala Hospital, had already stirred something in her blood and made her feel more alive. There was a sense of adventure here she had almost forgotten how to feel—a challenge.

She realised that they were drawing to a halt. A shabby-looking man in long dusty trousers and a khaki shirt was standing waiting for them beside a large thorn tree which seemed to mark the place where a dusty track branched away from the asphalt road. He came up to the ambulance with a look of relief and a flood of excited dialect, and Rose spoke to him for a moment or two, sounding soothing. Then she and Kate got down to travel in the back of the ambulance, leaving the man to climb in beside the driver and give him directions as they branched off into the bush.

Since the back of the ambulance had frosted-glass windows, Kate couldn't see the rest of the journey— another two hours of jolting progress across ground much rougher than the main road had been. Rose told her as they went that the mother had actually delivered in the early hours of this morning after a long labour, and something had gone wrong with the delivery so that the village grandmothers didn't know what to do. They hadn't actually thought of calling the hospital earlier, and the mother had never attended any ante-natal clinics—a fact which made Rose click her tongue in exasperation.

They pulled up at last. Kate picked up the bulky brown-paper parcel which was the delivery pack— bowls, instruments and a dressing-towel wrapped firmly in thick brown paper, sellotaped, and then autoclaved whole so that everything would be sterile when unwrapped—and stepped out into the sunlight as the ambulance's rear doors opened.

She saw that they had drawn up on the edge of a

village settlement which was made up of round huts, looking as if they were built of mud, each with a conical thatched roof on top and no windows so that there was only a doorway to let in light. The ground was dusty and a few small children stood staring round-eyed, dressed in tattered-looking T-shirts with nothing on their bottom halves. A skinny hen which had been rooting in the dust fluttered off with a squawk.

They were led swiftly among the huts, now, on the beaten-down earth which must have been cleared from the surrounding scrub, and Kate didn't have time to gather more than an impression of what she supposed, wonderingly, must be a typical Lanbwena village.

Three or four men stood around looking awkward outside one of the huts, as if they had been firmly excluded from it. Kate and Rose were signed to go in, and Kate had to adjust her eyes to the immediate dimness inside. The floor was earth, and so were the walls, and there were bundles and pots lying about, rather than furniture.

A woman straightened up with a quick jabber of speech, while two others stood to one side as if acting as sentinels, but it was the young woman on the floor who took Kate's attention at once. She was lying uncovered on the bare earth, very still, with a pallor visible even against her dark skin. Her eyes were closed. Beside her lay the baby with its cord still attached and leading into the mother. The placenta hadn't come away, that much was plain, and the older women hadn't separated the baby off after the incomplete birth. As she moved to it quickly, Kate found with relief that it was still alive. Chilled, even in this warm atmosphere, but still viable.

Afterwards, Kate found it hard to believe that she had worked so coolly. Rose's calm acceptance of the situation certainly helped, and the two of them were rapidly a team, checking on the mother, to find her cold but with a weak, fast pulse. They gave her a syntosinon injection to try to express the placenta and separated the baby and wrapped it up quickly to keep it warm.

The grandmother—at least, Kate assumed she must be the grandmother—produced a blanket which did seem to be clean, and which went round the baby on top of the green dressing-towel they had brought with them. There was a brief argument with the older woman, who seemed to feel that the baby ought to be washed, but she was rapidly convinced that warmth was more important and was usefully expert, then, in cradling the tiny creature against her own body while the two midwives set out to see what they could do for the mother.

A second injection of syntosinon still didn't produce the placenta so they decided to set up a dextrose drip to try to improve the young mother's condition. Already, it had stopped seeming unnatural to Kate to be setting up a drip in a hut. That done, they had a pause for discussion. It wasn't feasible simply to load her into the ambulance, because the jolting journey might easily cause her to haemorrhage. Rose gave Kate a doubtful look.

'Manual removal of the placenta, do you think? To be honest, it's not something I've had to do very often.'

'All the same, I think it's the best bet.' Kate hesitated, then offered, 'I'll do it if you like, while you hold the drip bottle up?'

They set to work carefully, after making things as sterile as possible with towels. Kate didn't have time to think how unlike her past experience it was. She only let herself remember that she had done this before successfully and it was part of her trained profession. Moments later she was looking up at Rose with a sigh of relief, and Rose gave her an answering grin.

By the time they loaded the mother into the ambulance, her condition already seemed to be improving. The grandmother was to travel with them and was still cradling the baby. Half the village seemed to have come out to see them off, with smiles all round. Kate was just returning a toddler to its mother to keep it away from the ambulance wheels, and giving the wriggling baby an involuntary hug as she handed it over because it was looking at her with such round-eyed wonder, when she was suddenly aware of the sound of a car driving up and drawing to a sharp halt.

She couldn't look round for a moment because the child had caught its fingers in the coil of her hair, as if drawn by curiosity to its fairness. She disentangled the small fingers carefully and tried to look reproving as he tugged at the long strand he had loosened.

'Why, Dr Kyle! I didn't know they were sending a doctor out after us, or we'd have waited,' Rose said in surprise.

'No, it's my day off, but I saw the ambulance and stopped to see if any help was wanted. I've been visiting one of the village schools a few miles from here.' As Kate managed to turn round, at last, she felt his eyes on her and hastily tried to tuck the loose piece of hair back into neatness. Seeing him standing there looking sun-bronzed and casual made her aware that she must look crumpled and shiny-faced, probably even a little grubby from kneeling on the hut floor. He went on, 'Any problems, or have you managed?'

'I think we're all right now, thank you,' Rose answered, smiling at him. 'Nurse Raven was with me, luckily, which was a great help. But if you want to check, of course—'

'No, I'll trust your judgment. I just stopped on the off-chance.' He glanced at Kate. There was, she decided, a thoughtful look in his eyes. For a defensive moment she thought he was going to say something dry, but instead he returned Rose's smile and said, 'You midwives are the experts on village deliveries, so I won't interfere with protocol by offering help if you don't need it! I just saw the ambulance parked, that's all. If you're all loaded up and ready, I won't hold you up. You've got quite a way to go!'

He stood holding the ambulance door as Kate walked across to climb in, and again she could feel his eyes assessing her, making her feel self-conscious as she passed him quickly and climbed inside. A moment later the doors were shut and the engine was starting. Kate felt suddenly, ridiculously, that it was unfair of him to stand there looking so handsome and casually tidy and thoroughly *at home* in the bush—and at the same time caught herself thinking just as foolishly that it would have been nice to be able to smile at him as Rose had, and share with him the glow of triumph she had been feeling over their success with the delivery . . .

There was no time to dwell on that as they moved off, with Rose carefully steadying the dextrose bottle which she had tied to a stanchion above the young mother's head. Kate exchanged smiles with the grand-mother as she balanced herself in her seat, and made a quick check with her finger against the infant's cheek to make sure that he had warmed up satisfactorily. He had. In fact he looked a remarkably healthy little specimen, considering all he'd been through. The mother, too, was stirring a little now and beginning to take an interest in her surroundings. Her pulse was distinctly stronger when Kate leaned over to check it, while Rose murmured some soothing words.

'That was like Dr Kyle, to leave it to us once I'd told him things were all right,' Rose said approvingly. 'Though if he'd turned up earlier, we'd have been glad of his advice, wouldn't we? I expect he'll stay in the village now, and check on the health of the children, even though it is supposed to be his day off.'

'Does he often hold unofficial clinics? I mean—I've heard he was doing some research of his own.'

'Yes, he's very hard-working. Lanji Jeriku—do you

know Dr Jeriku?—says he's one of the few Europeans the villagers will really talk to, because they feel he understands them.' Rose glanced round to make a check on their patient and to see that the drip was functioning properly, and added, 'Well, that was quite a nasty one, wasn't it? I do wish they'd call us in earlier!'

'I was going to ask you if they were always as bad as that!'

'Oh no, not nearly. It's usually more a question of leaving it too late to come in, rather than complications.' She glanced up at Kate with a smile. 'You didn't seem too worried about it, anyway. Were you? I was very glad to have you there, as I told Dr Kyle. I might have been landed with Maud, who's such a slowcoach and has to be told everything twice! Besides, the trainees are still getting their experience. But of course, you've done all of it before, which makes life so much easier!'

Kate certainly hadn't done all that before, but she couldn't help feeling a glow of pleasure from Rose's compliment. And, unwarily, an extra glow from the fact that Nicholas Kyle had been told. Had turned up, for once, when she was doing something right. Not, of course, that his opinion mattered . . .

She found herself wanting to draw Rose out some more on the subject of Nicholas Kyle, but the other girl was going through the instruments now and checking that nothing had been left behind. And besides, Kate certainly didn't wish to sound as if she was particularly interested in him; so she couldn't think why curiosity should suddenly have struck her.

They reached the hospital without further crises, though the journey back seemed longer, if thankfully smoother, than the trip out. The driver was obviously being extra-careful with his load on board.

Their patient and her baby were swiftly admitted and a blood-sample sent at once for cross-matching so that the mother could have her transfusion changed from dextrose to whole blood. The baby boy was washed and weighed and docketed and put into a crib in the Prem Unit for the moment, so that he could be given special observation.

Kate was quite startled to realise that she had been away from the hospital for hours, and had had nothing to eat either, so she was grateful when Sister sent her off to the canteen and told the two midwives that she would take their full report afterwards. And by the time this was done, Kate found herself going off duty more than an hour late. Time had passed quickly while they were in the village, and of course there had been the hours of travelling too.

She drove back to Dendaa with a feeling of exhilar-ation, though it was oddly mixed with a vague feeling of dissatisfaction, as if restlessness were setting her on edge. She told herself quickly that it was only because she was in a strange place, and away from the company of nurses she knew and with whom she could have got together to share her experiences of the day. Still, she could tell Tessa all about it—and about the Herero, too, and the sight of them on the road, which seemed a long time ago now.

But Tessa was out, and didn't come in all through the long evening. Perhaps she was working again. Or perhaps she was out with her beloved Nick, and hearing all about *his* day.

Kate told herself off for feeling injured about it and washed her hair in case any insects might have fallen into it from the hut roof under which she had spent so much of her day. Leaving it loose to dry, she wandered out into the small garden, and then came in again in response to the unexpected chill in the air, which took over as soon as the sun went down. It went down slowly, which was a surprise. She had always thought there were no sunsets in Africa, just a sudden dark. Richard Cranshaw could have told her things like that . . .

If only *he* lived in Dendaa too, instead of having rooms at the university, she could have gone out and wandered around in the hope of meeting him. But, of course, he might be working. He probably was. She couldn't imagine him being anything but studious. That was one of the things she'd always admired about him—unlike the Nicholas Kyles of this world who, however hard Rose Angkina might say he worked, couldn't really be anything but social.

Kate felt the familiar annoyance which the thought of him brought, and tossed her head. Then she paused, catching sight of herself in the mirror. The long, almost silver-blonde hair hanging round her face and reaching half-way down her back, instead of done up in its habitual neat coil or plaited to stop it tangling while she slept, made her look and feel different. It suited her mood. She was not prim, whatever Tessa might say!

She had every reason to dislike Nicholas Kyle, anyway, for what he had said to her. It wasn't just that he was tall and lean and undeniably good-looking, with an obvious charm—and besides, he was probably a womaniser like her father.

She knew, uncomfortably, that she had been pushing away the shock of hearing him mention her father all these past days. It had been a shock, too, to be told that she might have been expected to go to her father's funeral and to hear that he had been happy with the woman he'd married. Nicholas Kyle's aunt. Hadn't she been called Norma? Her mother had always referred to her as 'that woman'.

It was nothing to do with the present anyway, Kate thought defiantly. It wasn't anyone's business to remind her of the letters which had stopped coming because she never answered them. Nor, for that matter, of the tears she had cried so many nights as a child. How could *he* know what it was like to be torn two ways—or what it felt like to be taught to think badly of someone?

She put a block on her thoughts quickly and picked up a textbook. There was absolutely no reason to feel the sting of tears now. It would be far better to try to learn up some tropical diseases. After all, she was grown up now, a useful citizen and a good nurse—as Nicholas Kyle would find out. And why should she care what he thought of her, anyway? She certainly wasn't going to ask him all the questions she suddenly wanted to ask about her father, or let him see her longings . . .

She was schooled in hiding her feelings, and it was just as well for he was the first person she came across when she entered the Maternity Unit the next morning. Otherwise she might have shown surprise when he gave her an unexpectedly friendly look and said coolly, 'I hear you did well yesterday. Oh yes, I do give credit where credit's due, believe it or not!'

The last words held his usual sardonic undertone, but he had gone before she could think up a reply. He had looked tired and unshaven, as if he had been up most of the night—as he had, she learned afterwards, having come on duty at midnight to be faced with a nasty road accident requiring surgery, and then been called to a crisis on the medical side when a patient was admitted in cardiac arrest. He had come into Maternity as an extra, just to make an early-morning round of the new mothers and babies.

Well, she would have to admit that he did work hard and that he could still retain his air of attraction even with a morning growth of blond beard giving his handsome face a slightly raffish air. Not that he was Kate's type, or could ever be, she reminded herself quickly. It was annoying that she had even noticed it.

She had some days off coming up, so at least she would be out of his way, even if he had suddenly decided to criticise her less. The pattern of work, which was five days on and two off, or four nights on and three off on night duty, had already given her one spell of free time which she had spent partly on her own exploring Mutala, and partly with Tessa when her friend wasn't working,

This time she found herself unexpectedly invited to make a trip into South Africa with one of their Dendaa neighbours, travelling by car all the long miles down to Mafeking to see the Boer War Museum down there. Going back on duty for her next spell, Kate could begin to feel that she was becoming quite an African resident and she felt warmed by the friendliness of the Barker family, who had invited her on the trip with them and treated her as one of themselves.

They were quite new to Lanbwe too, having arrived just before Kate, so that they were all able to share in the fascination of Lanbwe's huge flatness, its widely-scattered villages, the strangeness of one road and one railway-line crossing an entire country, without her feeling strange and ignorant and such a newcomer that she must keep quiet about her impressions. Even with Richard, whom she hadn't seen again yet, she felt self-consciously aware of her lack of knowledge about a continent with which he must now be familiar, and afraid of saying something stupid. Not, of course, that he would rake her down for her ignorance, as Nick Kyle would.

She wasn't sure when she had started thinking of him as Nick rather than Nicholas, though perhaps it was just because Tessa always referred to him that way—and Sister, when she was in an informal mood. It suited him, too. Not that Kate cared what suited him. She had firmly decided not to think about him at all, when she could avoid it. She had enough to do getting used to the Maternity Unit without bothering about any particular doctors—though she had met quite a few of those by now.

She certainly wasn't thinking about any of the doctors when she stormed into the Unit on her second afternoon back on duty. She had been down to Old Katedi to visit a mother she had delivered ten days before, and on the way back had picked up her post from the private box in town she and Tessa now shared.

It had been bad enough to find that in Old Katedi, Mutala's one slum area in the remains of the original village which had been there before Mutala proper was built, there were only stand-pipes for water and the baby was being bottle-fed without that water being sterilised; it had been frustrating trying to talk to the mother through an interpreter and feeling that she really wasn't getting through to her. All that had been wiped out of her mind, though, when she paused to open her post and skimmed through a letter from her mother. It had been a long wail, urging Kate to come home at once. She couldn't do that, of course, however much Mrs Raven might need comforting, but she could feel a sudden rage and a returning knowledge of betrayal.

Somehow, at this moment, it wasn't even possible to remember how she'd always prided herself on keeping an efficiently cool exterior whenever she was on duty.

Her heels clicked angrily as she came into the ward, and she ignored the trainee who was dealing with an admission by the desk and who glanced round to give her a tentative smile. She had better find Sister to report her return, she supposed—or whichever of the other staff nurses was in charge of the ward at the moment. There were curtains drawn in various parts of the Unit and she felt suddenly inclined to take refuge in the Prem Room first, because there at least she could take comfort from the sight of the tiny babies nestling under their protective covers without having to try to smile and look normal. She swept on into the Prem Room—and found a young trainee in there. The girl flinched at the sight of Staff Nurse Raven and her flashing blue-eyed glare. It only made things worse.

'Where's Sister?' she snapped, for something to say.

'She's—she's off duty, I think, Staff Nurse.'

'Oh? Well, why is this room in such a mess? You should have tidied it up the minute you'd finished with the feeding mothers! What's your name? Ferula, isn't it?' It was, and she was the newest and most uncertain of the trainees, as well as being the only one Kate had met so far with an African first-name. Kate was in no mood to be fair at this moment and she had opened her mouth to tell Ferula off for standing about looking nervous when at that moment a male voice spoke behind her on a cold note.

'Ferula, would you go down to Admissions? Don't worry about things in here, Staff Nurse Raven can manage to deal with this room.'

The girl scuttled out. The door closed behind her and Nicholas Kyle leaned against it with his grey eyes cold and angry.

'So this is how you behave when you think no one's looking? And I thought you were showing signs of being better than I might have expected! Showing your temper on duty, Nurse, is highly unprofessional—and it's not the way to behave when you're new here, and working in a situation where foreigners are only tolerated. You can either pull yourself together, or I'm going to send you off duty.'

CHAPTER FOUR

IT WAS A long time since Kate had been spoken to as if she was the lowest pupil-nurse, and the shock of it made her gulp. The accusation of being unprofessional stung, too. She glared at him with acute dislike. It had to be *him*, of all people.

'I don't usually show my temper,' she said resentfully, trying to keep the shake out of her voice. 'And I—I don't think you can complain about my work, either, however much you'd like to.'

'You'd better tell me what's upsetting you. You look,' he said sardonically, 'as if someone's been rash enough to make a pass at you on your way in—or as if you've mistaken someone's friendly greeting for that!'

'Oh, don't be ridiculous!' It might not be the way she was supposed to speak to a doctor on the ward, but his presence was the worst irritant she could have found. 'If you'll just leave me alone,' she said icily, 'I'll be perfectly all right. Just—'

'No. Your behaviour's my business, so you can explain it,' he said uncompromisingly. 'I'd just finished examining my patient when I looked out through the curtains and saw you moving through the ward looking like a hurricane in search of someone to batter. I've got the time. Well?'

'My behaviour's not your business.' A prem, stirring under its cover, reminded Kate where she was and made her moderate her voice quickly, searching for control. He was still standing there, and the reminder of what he represented made her come out with it, whether she would or not, in a much lower voice but a cold one just the same. 'Oh, very well, Dr Kyle. If you want to know what's upset me, I've just had a letter from my mother. About my father's estate, if you must know, and the fact that it's finally been wound up. I'm sure it wouldn't mean anything to *you* that he died without even considering her at all, but—'

'Oh?' He was watching her now, with a kind of clinical interest, and with one eyebrow raised. 'You did grow up to be a materialist, on top of everything else, didn't you?'

'No!' Kate said rapidly, furious at the accusation. The prem stirred again, and it was good to have an excuse to move and look down at the infant to hide the uncomfortable sting his words gave her, and her inclination to blink on tears, too. She was in control of herself by the time she looked up at him again and continued with a false calm, though with a dull, angry glow in her stomach. '*I'm* not bothered one way or the other if he left everything to his new family,' she said coldly. 'It really doesn't make any difference to me! But my mother's naturally upset that—that—'

'That he died intestate without leaving her anything? How inconsiderate of him to die so suddenly, wasn't it?' There was a heavy note of sarcasm in his voice. 'It was inconvenient for his new family too, in case you hadn't thought of that—let alone the fact that *they* were genuinely upset by it! What's your mother worrying about? Loss of maintenance? Hasn't she got a job? Good God, they've been divorced for all of—what— fourteen years? Yes, it must be, because Michael's twelve and John's—'

'Thank you, but I really don't want to know about—'

'Your half-brothers? No, you wouldn't, would you? After all, you've never shown the slightest interest in them until now.' He eyed her caustically, but with a sudden glimmer of understanding as she bristled involuntarily. Kate felt as if the room had grown suddenly much too small. He began, thoughtfully, 'You really never needed to be jealous, if that's it.'

'No, it certainly isn't!' Kate retorted. She wasn't having him thinking *that*, nor that she had cared one way or the other. Why should she care if her father had had the sons he always wanted; if 'that woman' had provided them, as her mother so often bewailed? She certainly wasn't going to stand for a look of unexpected sympathy from the member of the Kyle family standing in front of her. 'We were talking about my mother,' she said icily, 'and the fact that she—she's suddenly losing part of her income because he—he—'

It was damnable of him to stand watching her in a way that made her stammer uncomfortably. It was damnable, too, to have to remember that Mrs Raven was actually quite well-off. Particularly, the betraying thought nudged at her, in comparison with the standard of living out here, where the poor were so incredibly poor that it was outside Western comprehension.

'Oh, I don't know why I'm talking to you about it at all!' she said quickly, angrily drawing the rags of her dignity around her. 'You're not likely to have any sympathy, are you?'

'Hardly. What would you have expected me to do? Put my arms round you and say there, there and offer to kiss you better?' He said that with his eyebrows raised and with a warning look when she immediately stiffened. 'No, I wasn't planning to, so you needn't flinch away in that outraged fashion!'

'I certainly didn't—'

'Think I would? Oh, but I might, if you were any other pretty girl being unreasonably upset over family matters! Unreasonable, because a man can't really be blamed for dying of a sudden heart attack without leaving a will, now can he? Even if his relatives are left not knowing whether he ever thought about them or not.' He was sounding much too thoughtful and

Kate opened her mouth to make some angry retort—but before she could do so he went on. 'But I'll bet Norma's spared more concern for *you* over your father's death, and the way you might be feeling, than you've ever spared her. And there really isn't any question of sympathy between you and me, is there? We're thoroughly on opposite sides of the fence.'

'It's time I got back to work,' Kate said sharply, wishing he wasn't between her and the door so that she could sweep out of the room and put as much space as possible between them. 'And didn't you say, Dr Kyle, that you were in the middle of examining a patient? I don't think we should be standing here discussing personal matters.'

'Then don't bring personal matters on duty with you,' he said drily, though he did begin to move his shoulders away from the door-frame. 'And I said I'd just *finished* examining a patient, as it happens. Sister may be tolerant, but I doubt if she'd have put up with you banging about and scowling and causing an atmosphere! So remember what I said, and stay in here until you can come out looking calm and quiet and more like a nurse.'

'Yes, Dr Kyle,' Kate said between her teeth, and blanking her face with an effort of will because she knew, however unwillingly, that he had a right to tell her off. Over professional matters. It was lucky the prems were drowsy and recently fed, too, she thought with a sudden sense of guilt, because tiny babies were all too good at sensing tension in the air. She should have thought of that before she brought her temper in here with her. She wished Nick Kyle would actually go, and let her steady herself properly.

And he was going, thank goodness, even if he was taking his time about it. He had turned back to study her, with his hand on the door-knob. Approvingly, he said, 'You know, you're an interesting girl, Cousin

Kate. Not altogether as uptight as I thought. And, usually, much better at working here than I was expecting you to be! Oh yes, I *had* noticed!'

He was opening the door as he spoke, and a moment later he had gone, leaving her fuming. And confused. How dare he call her Cousin Kate like that, and sound almost friendly about it too, after all they had just been saying? If ever anyone could be more maddening . . .

She shook herself, and looked quickly round the Prem Room, trying to feel calm enough to start tidying it up without moving too briskly and disturbing the sleepy babies. With luck he would have left by the time she went out into the Unit again.

Her mother's letter crackled in her pocket as she turned, and the reminder brought an uncomfortably guilty feeling that he had been right in some of the things he had said. Her mother didn't actually need the money, however much she might complain that she did. In fact she'd had plenty ever since Kate's maternal grandparents had died. Even her letter had made it sound more like a matter of principle. It had been one more score to set against 'that woman', and there hadn't been a word to wonder about whether the other Raven family needed provision more than she did. Or whether they might miss him. And it *had* been fourteen years . . .

Kate wrenched her mind away and made herself think about work instead of about the scorn in a pair of grey eyes. In fact it was a relief to cast her mind back to what she had been doing before all this blew up; to remind herself of the home visit to Old Katedi this afternoon, and the determination it had brought her to learn at least a smattering of Lanbwena as soon as possible. She wasn't going to be defeated by her lack of language if she could help it—particularly not in her care for the babies it was her job to bring into the world. Dr Nick Kyle might find that surprising, she thought bitterly, but then he didn't know her, however well he might think he did!

She didn't know why she had to let him disturb her so much. She certainly didn't care about his approval or disapproval. She knew she was good at her job, and besides, she had just as much right to be here as he did. Coming off duty some time later, congratulating herself that she had completed the afternoon with a quiet efficiency, she found herself wishing that she hadn't finished work for the day. She really didn't want time to think.

She suddenly found herself with a defiant longing to drive over to the university. It was only four o'clock, since she had been on the morning shift again. She had the excuse of asking Tessa whether there was such a thing as a Lanbwena phrase-book which she could then go back into Mutala to buy. And she could suggest stocking the refrigerator for the next few evening meals, while she was shopping. And, besides—

Besides, there was one person who had said it was an excellent idea that she had come to Mutala. The one person whose approval she really did want.

The university wasn't far, since Mutala itself wasn't large. It was a small, modern campus set on the opposite edge of the town from the hospital. Its glass-fronted buildings reminded her of one of the newer comprehensive schools and it wasn't difficult to find out where Professor Cranshaw and his assistant worked, because there was a porter on duty. Kate found the upstairs corridor to which she had been directed and hesitated a little, her heart beating suddenly faster at the sight of an open laboratory door at the end of the corridor. It was silly to be suddenly seized with shyness. Hadn't he said that she must come up to the university some time?

She was passing an open office door, and her attention was immediately caught by the figure seated at the desk.

Richard . . . Not in the lab, as she had automatically
expected to find him, but frowning over some papers
on the desk in front of him, with his narrow face screwed
up in concentration and one lock of dark hair flopping
over his face. She had seen him look like that before,
so there was no reason why it should suddenly be like
looking at a total stranger. Older, somehow, when the
blue short-sleeved shirt he was wearing should really
have made him look younger than the professorial suit
and tie she remembered him in best. At that moment
he looked up, frowning, and caught sight of her.

'I'm sorry,' she said quickly, 'I didn't mean to disturb
you.'

'Oh, it's Kate! Are you looking for Tessa?' He glanced
round abstractedly before bringing his eyes back to her
face, and then began to get to his feet with quick
courtesy. 'No, you're not really disturbing me. I thought
for a moment I was back in the hospital in London,
seeing a figure in uniform!'

'I'm on my way off duty,' Kate told him quickly,
feeling inclined to give him a maternal smile for his
inevitable vagueness, which always made him look
remarkably helpless for a man of his talents. She found
that he was waiting politely for her to say something
else.

'I—I hope it doesn't matter, my dropping in?'

'No, not at all. It's very nice to see you,' he said
promptly. 'How are you enjoying being in Lanbwe?
The hospital's rather a contrast for you after St John's,
I should imagine? I suppose it's rather odd that there
should be three of us out here, all from St John's,
exchanging tradition for the Third World.'

'Yes, I—I suppose so. That's an unusual photograph,
isn't it?' Kate said hastily. She could hardly blurt out
that she had come here to see him, could she? She felt
a wave of embarrassment which made her move quickly
to look at the enlargement pinned on the wall. 'Is it an

unusual racial mix or something? Surely you don't often see ginger hair on an African child, do you?'

'Ah, so you haven't come across the typical "kwashiorkor look"?' he asked, making her feel foolish, but moving round the desk to point out certain features of the photograph to her. He didn't sound critical of her ignorance, though, as he went on to explain that it was malnutrition which rusted the pigmentation of the hair and caused pale blotches on the skin. 'What we're trying to do is to make a thorough survey of it, to see whether it's solely nutrition or whether there's some other factor involved in the body-changes which occur. Now this one, which we found in Ghana, showed particularly . . .'

He went on to explain it to her, and she told herself that it was flattering that he should take the trouble. Even if he was telling her more than she could readily understand, she could listen to him respectfully and feel how valuable his work must be. Besides, she was standing beside him, wasn't she? And—the thought crept into her mind with a feeling of defiance—it was nice to be treated like somebody intelligent. To feel safe and secure and appreciated and—

'There are quite a few more pictures I could show you to illustrate the varying effects,' Richard Cranshaw said, bringing her back abruptly to the present. 'Unfortunately, the best ones haven't been sorted out yet.' He paused to smile at her, though there was a touch of annoyance in his eyes. 'If,' he said, frowning again, 'my recent assistant's work hadn't only just arrived back with us, and done up in such an unholy jumble that I can't find anything in it until it's been properly collated, I could have shown you photographs to illustrate the chain I was describing! Dr Harvey enclosed a letter assuring me that everything was dated, and apologising for taking the whole lot away by mistake—but since a quick glance through shows that none of the dates are actually in order, she's landed us with an extra and quite unnecessary job!'

He sounded so irritated that the smile Kate had been giving him died and she put on a meekly sympathetic expression. His glance towards a bulging package on the filing cabinet had indicated the cause of the problem, and she wondered wryly how many extra evenings of work that meant for Tessa. And then another idea occurred to her, and she found herself saying,

'Is it a very difficult job? I mean, does it require much technical knowledge?'

'No, a filing clerk could do it, if the university could spare us one. Unfortunately they can't, and Tessa seems to feel rather overloaded at the moment.'

'Then perhaps I could help? If it's really a job anyone could do,' Kate said quickly. 'Couldn't I? I do have days off—or there's evenings.'

'Would you really be prepared to do that? How very nice of you!' He was looking at her with so much approval that she almost flushed. 'Well, if you're really sure. And since I know you're trustworthy, you could take them home, instead of having to bother to come here. That really would be very useful of you!'

It wasn't what Kate had visualised when she made the impulsive offer, but he was turning away to pick up the package and hand it to her, and murmuring, 'We must give you a file to put everything in—I'm sure Tessa must have one somewhere.'

'I've got one of *what* somewhere?' Tessa's voice said from the doorway, making Kate jump. 'Oh, hallo, Katie, I didn't know you were here. In fact I wondered who it was R.J. was talking to. What are you doing with those *now*?'

It wasn't a surprise to hear Tessa refer to the Professor by his initials, since she had used them once or twice before in letters. It shouldn't have been surprising to hear her use them to his face either, after the informality of two years of travelling round Africa together. It *was* a little startling to hear her address him in a reproving tone which had a distinct crossness in it, and to see that she was glowering at him in a way which he seemed too politely tolerant to notice.

'Kate's offered to sort out Dr Harvey's notes for us. That's extremely helpful of her, isn't it? So perhaps you'd find her something to put them in? And thank you again, Kate, or is it always Katie?' he added with a sudden sweet smile and a concentrated interest which almost made her blush again. 'I wonder which suits you better? Oh dear, *now* who wants me?'

The last was in response to a sudden bleep from the telephone on his desk. As he turned away to answer it, Kate found that Tessa was drawing her away out of the room, muttering gruffly, 'Come on, I was tidying the lab, and that's probably the Dean of the medical school calling him again. Honestly, I don't know how we're supposed to get on with anything if he will keep letting himself be distracted—'

She was still sounding uncommonly cross. She shut the door of the empty lab behind the two of them.

'It's too bad of him to dump that lot on you! Look, give the wretched things to me, and I'll point out to him that you do have a job of your own to do! You shouldn't let him.'

'It's all right, I offered! He said you were overloaded,' Kate said hastily, hoping that her flush didn't betray her, 'so I offered to help. I'm sorry, it never occurred to me that you'd mind.'

'Oh, I don't! It's just that he's been awful about them ever since they arrived.' Tessa had the grace to look slightly shamefaced. She even tried to give Kate a grin. 'As a matter of fact, he's been awful all today,' she said aggressively. 'He can be thoroughly unreasonable.'

'Can he? I thought he was being particularly nice. He's just explained kwashiorkor to me in detail.' Kate tried to still the sudden happiness she was feeling in the face of her friend's obviously bad mood, and added lightly, 'I did wonder if you always spoke to him like that!'

'No, I don't, actually, only he's been so *picky*—' Tessa gave Kate a look from under her brows, and then made an obvious effort to pull herself together. She even managed to produce a gleam of humour. 'I suppose I just thought he was taking it out on me for saying I was too busy to do Dr Harvey's notes yet, but if you really offered—'

'I did. I might as well try to stop you being over-worked, mightn't I?' Kate said cheerfully, and then felt a touch of guilt at the pretence, since it hadn't actually been Tessa she had in mind at all. To cover it she looked down hastily at the package she was clutching, and added, 'He said he only wanted it all put in date order, and I suppose I'll be able to read it all right!'

'Oh yes, she had nice writing, to go with all her other perfections! No, you're right, I didn't like her much,' Tessa said defensively at Kate's look of surprise. 'Though that wasn't why I didn't want to sort out her notes! In fact I'd rather have the extra work than have her around. Oh, take no notice, I'm being thoroughly stupid today!'

'Goodness, was she really that bad?'

'No, I s'pose not, and at least she's gone,' Tessa said, looking suddenly more cheerful. 'But don't ask me what she was like, because she was just too—oh, too everything! Nick used to call her "Venus" if that gives you any idea! What did you come for, Katie, in the first place? Sorry, I should have asked you, instead of running on like that.'

'Just to see if there was any shopping I should do,' Kate said quickly, remembering her excuse and trying not to show that she had jumped at Nick's name. She tried not to give her friend a comprehending glance, too. If Tessa could show jealousy merely at the thought of the departed Dr Harvey, she really *had* got it bad for Nick Kyle.

Not that it was Kate's business, she told herself quickly, except that the man acted like a rasp on her nerves, and made a habit of looking at her as if she'd crawled out from under a stone, and . . . She decided rapidly not to make a catalogue of Nick Kyle's dislike for her, which was definitely mutual. And not to feel dispirited about it, either.

'I thought I could get something in for supper tonight,' she began. But at that moment the lab door opened and Richard Cranshaw was with them again.

'Ah, you're still here,' he said, giving Kate a smile. And then to Tessa, 'We must get Kate a ticket for the University Open Day Dance next month. It suddenly occurred to me while I was talking to the Dean. Would you like to come, Kate?'

'I thought you said you were going to make the excuse of going to Johannesburg then so as not to have to attend?'

'Oh, I think I shall go, after all. We can fit in Johannesburg some time before then, can't we? I'm afraid it means joining an official party,' he said, smiling at Kate, 'but at least we can lower the average age of it with you and Tessa there, can't we? And, besides, you might find it entertaining!'

'Yes, I would, thank you.'

'Good,' he said pleasantly, and wandered out again, leaving her with a feeling of disbelief. And a hasty review of her wardrobe, trying to think if she had packed anything remotely suitable for attending an official function with Richard. Had he really walked in like that and so particularly asked her?

She was suddenly aware that Tessa's face had gone oddly blank. Oh dear, she must have been hoping to go with Nick. And now it had just been made clear to her

that if her employer went, *she* had to be part of the
official party too. Kate had to stifle her own feeling of
triumph and hope with quick self-consciousness, so that
she didn't look as if she was beaming with happiness
when her friend was so obviously cast down. Tessa had
turned away to fiddle with something on a bench and
was speaking abruptly over her shoulder.

'It's not for another four weeks, so at least your
trunk's sure to have come by then. I was going to ask
if you wanted to come, anyway. Most people will, since
we don't have much in the way of entertainments. Well,
there's the occasional film show held in the lecture hall
here, but they aren't usually up to much.'

'Tess?'

'Oh yes, something to get for supper. I expect you
want to get home, don't you?' Tessa had turned round
now, with a sudden briskness which discouraged Kate
from anything she might have been going to say. 'And
I've got to find you a file, haven't I? Don't bother about
supper for me. I—I think I promised to babysit for
someone, and there's no point in my coming home first.
You can get a chicken to cook for tomorrow, if you
want one—I'll probably be in then.'

Tessa had always been extremely private about her
feelings. It was part of her shyness, and even with Kate
she had sometimes clammed up and looked defensive.
Like now. A friendly but mutual privacy had made
sharing easy in the old days, and if Tessa seemed to
have changed in some ways, she hadn't in that. Kate
knew better than to push her, and as she left a few
moments later she decided to cultivate her own bubble
of happiness instead. One, Richard had looked pleased
to see her; two, she had pleased him still further by
offering to do some work for him; three, and scarcely
believable, he had apparently suddenly decided to go
to the dance so that he could invite her to it!

She couldn't remember if he had ever been to the St

John's dances, even the formal functions. That was one reason why she'd always had to worship him from a distance. But of course it was different out here. As different already as she'd dreamed it might be.

She was too caught up in her thoughts to look where she was going, and when she rounded the corner at the foot of the stairs she bumped straight into someone. In fact she was so concerned not to drop the armful of notes she held that she more or less fell into his arms. She was caught and steadied and set back on her feet—and before she could tilt her head to look up with a swift apology, and all-too-familiar voice said drily,

'We do keep running into each other, don't we?'

'Oh . . .' She wasn't going to let even *his* presence spoil her feeling of well-being, Kate decided swiftly. In fact she was even going to think with uncommon charity that it would cheer Tessa up to see him. All the same, she disentangled herself from the steadying grasp of Nick Kyle's hands abruptly, with the feeling that they had seemed to burn through her arms even before she knew it was him. 'What are you doing here?' she asked.

'Visiting. And exchanging research information, if Richard's in. We do have related interests,' he answered her quite civilly. 'You were calling on Tessa, I suppose? And looking remarkably cheerful . . . You do change moods quickly, don't you?'

'I don't have to . . .'

'Bear grudges all day? I'm glad to hear it. You're even looking at me as if I might be almost human, which is surprising.'

She had been thinking exactly the same about him, so it was startling to hear him come out with it. It made her tilt her chin, wishing he wouldn't remind her. She wasn't in any mood to sort out the confusion inside her head.

'I hope all that stuff you're carrying doesn't mean Tessa's trying to catch up by taking work home?'

'No, it's something I've offered to do for—for her.'
Kate had almost said, 'for Professor Cranshaw,' with
the defiant feeling of showing him that someone, at
least, valued her. But she found she didn't quite dare
in the face of those alert grey eyes. Even when he wasn't
being critical he seemed to produce a kind of electricity
in the air which made her wish he wasn't standing so
close and blocking her way. She made to step round
him, but to her surprise he said abruptly,

'No, don't go. I was thinking that I might have mis-
judged you. Or rather, that I shouldn't have pre-judged
the issue on the strength of bias. Very bad clinical
practice, isn't it?'

'What?'

'How about a truce? If only for the sake of our mutual
friends,' he said quickly, and with the barest trace of
mockery back in his voice, as if he was aware of the
way she had stiffened. 'We can't go on spitting at each
other like cat and dog at irregular intervals, just because
of past history, can we?'

'*You* started it!'

'I did. I admit it. Not this afternoon, which we'll leave
aside for the moment, but when you first arrived. You
irritated me,' he said coolly, as if she was supposed to
accept that. And then, with an almost friendly air,
'But we don't have to go on making each other's lives
uncomfortable, do we? If we don't choose?'

The discomfort had all been one-sided as far as Kate
could see, though 'for the sake of our mutual friends'
obviously meant Tessa, and sounded suspiciously as if
Tessa might have relayed her remarks about him. Had
they even quarrelled over it, with Tessa feeling the need
to defend Kate, just as she had defended him? 'If you
mean you're apologising for being unfair,' she began
stiffly.'

'You mean for coming on at you like the Montagues
against the Capulets? I suppose I did a bit, didn't I?'

He was watching her with a quizzical expression. 'Oh go on, girl, relax, and accept an olive branch when it's offered to you!'

'Why?' Kate asked baldly. Surely it wasn't possible to forget the scorn in his face this afternoon, was it? Let alone all the things he had said to her when she first arrived.

'Oh, because it occurred to me that it was time to stop jumping in with both feet. And personally, I can get tired of atmospheres, particularly among people I have to work with.' He sounded impatient now, and certainly not at all apologetic, even if he seemed to be reining himself in. He also sounded as if he felt any bad atmosphere between them had come entirely from her—which might be true of today, but certainly wasn't true of any other day.

'If you mean you're going to stop picking on me in the Unit, that'll be fine by me,' Kate said, pointedly.

'If I have reason to tell you off over your job,' he said harshly, 'you'll know it, like this afternoon. But go on, if you really insist on making everyone's life difficult by standing on your dignity all the time, be like that!'

With that he did stand aside for her, throwing her a mocking look which wiped all the friendliness out of his face and left it set in a mask of disgust. She walked past him, simply because he was obviously waiting for her to go, and she found herself clutching the bundle of notes in her arms like a talisman, to remind her that *some* people didn't set out to goad her. Richard didn't, and it was Richard she was interested in. So why should she care what anyone else thought of her?

She had gone no more than a yard when Nick Kyle spoke again behind her.

'Cousin Kate! No, all right, *Kate!*' he called, as she swung round to glare at him. 'Yes, you're quite right, I did only do it to annoy you. You really are a thoroughly impossible girl, did you know that? Though, come to think of it, you really are quite different from the skinny kid with braces on her teeth and pigtails, which is the photo I remember of you best.'

'I thought you said you wanted a truce?' Kate said. 'And I thought you were accusing me of being the one who wouldn't accept it?'

'You're right. I'm as bad at making up as you are.' There was a glimmer of laughter in his eyes suddenly, and a self-mockery which was totally surprising. And he had said *she* changed moods suddenly! 'I'm having one last try,' he said, with a dangerous air, 'even if you do make me wonder why! I thought you might like to know that when Tessa asked me what I'd done to upset you, I didn't tell her. I don't go round discussing other people's private lives, in case you thought I did.'

'I didn't, as a matter of fact.'

'Good. Just because she's a friend of both of us, and a particularly sweet and loyal girl with it, doesn't mean she has to be landed in the middle of it. Well, are you going to accept the peace-pact I'm offering you? Since we do have to see each other at work—'

'And for the sake of our mutual friends?' Kate said sweetly. She couldn't imagine why she was letting him get away with it, except, of course, for Tessa's sake. She certainly wasn't going to feel hurt if he only bothered with her because of that. But just because he had decided to stop being an enemy didn't mean she had to like him. 'Is there anything else?' she asked.

'No,' he said, equally politely. 'That was all I wanted to say. I'll be seeing you in the Unit, though not too soon, you'll be glad to hear, since I'm off to Williamstown for a few days to do a surgical list for them. Don't do anything I wouldn't do, while I'm gone.'

He didn't have to add that, Kate thought crossly as she walked away, even if he had said it quite amiably. And she still didn't know why she had agreed to a truce, except that it hadn't been a war of her making in the first place. It would certainly be less tiring to have a good working relationship with him, as long as he meant to stick to it. He'd admitted twice today that she'd surprised him by being good at the job. Perhaps he hadn't actually been picking on her as much as she'd thought.

She found herself thinking involuntarily that Mutala Hospital would miss him while he was gone, and wondered how on earth such a short-staffed hospital managed to lend out its doctors when they were thin enough on the ground already. Well, it was presumably part of the system, and it was always possible that the small local hospital in Lanbwe's northern township didn't have a full-time doctor of its own at all. She wouldn't miss Nick Kyle, of course, except with relief, but the Maternity Unit would.

Anyway, she was off duty now, and she had Richard to dream about. So why think about anything else?

CHAPTER FIVE

'PUT OUT a call for a doctor for me, will you, Leah? And then would you come and explain to this mother that we aren't bringing her baby to her only because of the chest infection?'

Kate paused to make soothing motions to the mother who was propped upright, her breathing a heavy rasp, and tried again to get through to her in halting words of Lanbwena. She had been working hard on them over the last three weeks, getting the trainees to write down words and phrases for her and give her pronunciations. It was a pity, she thought absently, to have to drag the medical staff in at eleven o'clock at night, but this chest infection had worsened so fast that she really did need an antibiotic written up. And whoever came could look at the latest admission which, to Kate, felt suspiciously like a breech.

As she thought of the breech, she found herself hoping it would be Nick who came—or was he still away? He had been back once after his trip to Williamstown, but only briefly before he vanished again on another trip. Perhaps that was why Tessa still seemed moody, though Kate hadn't really seen much of her since joining the night duty roster, with its alternating one week of nights, one week of days. It had brought back her jumbled feeling to swop over like that, even if now, half-way through her second session, she was beginning to get used to it.

It had made time pass remarkably quickly too. She could scarcely realise that it was three weeks since that day at the university. Three remarkably peaceful weeks, apart from the rush of work. And three remarkably sociable weeks off duty, too, since the Dendaa families seemed to have adopted her with their easy expatriate friendliness. If she hadn't seen Richard because, when she returned Dr Harvey's notes after carefully putting them in order, she found she had chosen a time when he was closeted in a meeting, at least he had sent his particular thanks via Tessa. Anyway, she could wait to see him until the dance, which was only a week away now.

As Leah came back to take over from her, Kate moved up the ward making a mental check of everything in the Unit. The babies had been fed and settled, the post-natal mothers checked, and no one was in the second stage of labour just now. Perhaps they were going to have a nice quiet night. She hoped so.

The ward only ran to one staff midwife all night, and four trainees. Furthermore, if the staff midwife suddenly had to go on a call-out, she still had to be responsible for everything which might happen in her absence. Kate had felt a twinge of nervousness about that, although she had done two more day-time call-outs by now with only a trainee for company. But she told herself staunchly that she would manage, whatever happened.

Luckily, night call-outs seemed to be fairly rare, either through chance or good management. All the same, she hoped there wouldn't be one tonight if Nick still wasn't here for the trainees to call on. Not that he was the only doctor, she reminded herself quickly.

Besides, Kate didn't know why she should be so keen to see his return, when even thinking about him was an uncomfortable reminder of the letter she had written to her mother, full of careful briskness which wouldn't hold nearly as much sympathy as Mrs Raven would have been expecting. On the other hand, she could remember that on the occasions she had seen Nick since that day at the university, he had seemed remarkably inclined to keep to their truce and had smiled at her pleasantly, even if there had been a guarded look in his eyes.

She turned her head quickly as someone came in at the far end of the Unit, and then knew she shouldn't be feeling disapppointed because it was one of the Lanbwena doctors who had arrived in answer to their call. She moved to him quickly, stood beside him while he examined the bronchitis patient, and drew up an antibiotic injection for him after he had written it up on the patient's notes. Then she tried not to wish he would look less tentative as he tried to feel whether the other patient's baby was lying out of position or not. Kate could scarcely contradict him when he left saying he thought everything seemed normal, even if she still didn't think so. Now, if it had been Nick . . .

Night duty must be affecting her mind, she decided abruptly, if she could feel quite so bereft without him, just because he was a skilful doctor. She went down the ward to make sure all the patients were tucked up with blankets and that the lights were dimmed. It was much colder in the hospital at night, in contrast to the day-time heat, so that for once she had to think about keeping the mothers and babies warm instead of cool. That done, there were chores to be got through.

The Unit went on being quiet, and after a while there was time to catch up on writing notes. Kate settled down at the desk, under its shaded light, letting her eyes go round occasionally and wondering whether she had been wise to let two trainees go at once to second lunch. Still, even night nurses had to eat during the long shift from nine p.m. to eight a.m. and Isaac, who tended to worry a lot, would probably come back early. When the Unit door clicked softly behind her she didn't look round for a moment, until an unexpected voice said quietly,

'A night nurse in a halo of light. Now that is a classic

picture, isn't it? No, I'm not being sarcastic, so you needn't jump like that!'

'Oh, you're back,' Kate said involuntarily, and then wished she'd said, 'Good evening, Dr Kyle,' with proper formality, as she saw him standing there in the shadow behind her.

'Yes, this evening, and I've stopped being peripatetic for the moment. Which is a relief, I may say.' He was standing looking down at her, and she had a sudden odd awareness of the picture they must make—the tall fair doctor, and the equally fair nurse looking up at him, isolated together in the surrounding dimness.

At that moment he shifted his shoulders as if pulling himself back to attention, and said, 'Benu Desato said you were worrying about a patient, a new admission, so I thought I'd come and have a look. What's the problem, or has it already resolved itself? I've just got in and I was coming to have my usual wander round Maternity anyway, to see that it hadn't fallen down in my absence, so it isn't a criticism, if you were about to take it that way!'

'I wasn't. I might have asked if you always wandered round Maternity at one in the morning, though.' For once she wasn't going to rise to him, perhaps because he had sounded teasing rather than sardonic, and it seemed remarkably easy to smile at him as if there had never been anything between them. Kate pulled herself together quickly and tried to remember that although night duty might feel informal, she was still supposed to give him a proper report. 'I was concerned about a possible breech, Dr Kyle, although it isn't urgent because labour isn't very far advanced.

'But she's come in early to get a comfortable bed for the night?' He leaned over her shoulder to look at the notes she had been making on the file, and Kate was conscious of his warmth. She kept her eyes on the brown finger which ran quickly down the list of the patient's age, previous births and medical history, and wondered why she had to feel so over-aware of his closeness and of the way their bodies were almost touching. She could feel the vibrations of his voice as he said, 'No ante-natal notes on this one. I suppose she thought she wouldn't bother, when it's her fourth. Well, I'll go and take a look at her. No, you needn't come. One of us will make less of a disturbance than two!'

He straightened up and moved away, giving Kate an odd sense of relief. Relief because she valued his opinion, she told herself quickly, and glanced round the ward to make sure nothing else was needing her attention. No, because there was no one in the delivery room, and she didn't need to go and look again to make sure the sluice was tidy and the trainee she had left in charge of the prems was perfectly capable . . . And it would be foolish to start moving about and looking busy just because Nick was in the ward.

She bent her head to concentrate on Isaac's delivery report from earlier in the evening, which she must countersign, and even managed to read it with an effort. Her ears seemed to be tuned to the soft murmur of Nick's voice as he spoke to the patient, and she tried to blank it out. Then he was back beside her and pulling out a chair to sit down, relaxing his long length into it in a way which suggested weariness.

'Yes, you're right, though it might have been difficult to spot because it's a shoulder-presentation, isn't it?' he said amiably.'Too awkward a position to turn. I don't think she'll deliver before morning, but it's a good thing you noticed. I don't need to tell you to keep an eye on her for the rest of the night, do I?'

'No, Dr Kyle. Quarter-hourly observation?'

'Half-hourly will do to start off with. She seems pretty quiet. May I have your permission to sit down for five minutes, Staff Nurse?'

'Yes, of course.'

'Good, because you were giving me the oddest feeling I was disturbing you!'

'No—' Kate quickly quelled her impulse to stiffen in the face of the deliberately teasing look he was giving here. She *hadn't* been disturbed by his sitting down beside her, either. She had merely sat up a little straighter out of decorous habit because they were discussing a patient.

'I feel like a little company, as a matter of fact, and if I hide in here, nobody can catch me for any other emergency, can they? Particularly since I'm not really supposed to be on duty until tomorrow morning.' He stretched, grinning at her with a sudden open friendliness which was almost disconcerting. 'I've just spent a week going round the outlying clinics. You won't have seen any of those, will you? They're small, and mainly staffed by paramedics.'

'Do you often get called out to them?'

'It's a general round. We take it in turns to do it. I was mug enough to offer to take an extra turn, since it gives me the chance to follow up my own research.' He was making conversation quite casually, just as if they were any two people passing time together. When he yawned and then apologised, Kate felt an impulse to tell him sympathetically that he ought to go to bed. He did look tired.

'I do sometimes wonder why I bother,' he said ruefully, 'and whether it's actually going to make any difference if I write a paper on, oh, measles epidemics among the undernourished, or tubercle, which goes on presenting itself becasuse people don't like to admit to having it, or poor hygiene causing gastro-enteritis.'

'Somebody's got to care about it,' Kate said, because he was looking suddenly discouraged.

'Oh, plenty of people care about it! But that doesn't mean anything's going to improve overnight just because *I* write about it!'

'It might. Anyway, getting something published might help your career,' Kate offered.

'Oh, that. I should probably have stayed at home and opted for either obstetrics or paediatrics instead of being too interested in both. Or decided to quit hospitals altogether and go in for general practice.' He was looking moody all at once, and staring down at his hands as if he had forgotten who it was he was talking to. 'But instead I came to Africa . . . And serve me right for being restless, my family would say.' He glanced up quickly then, as if suddenly aware of her, and added, 'Take no notice, I'm tired. After all the driving I've been doing over non-existent roads, I ought to be. Besides,' he gave her a look into which an edge of mockery had come back, 'if I go on like that, you'll simply think I'm trying to put you off again, won't you?'

'No.' She wished he hadn't brought things back to that again, but had simply gone on talking. She wished that the grey eyes, so smoky that in this light they seemed almost black, wouldn't look at her so intently, too, making her feel as if he was seeing right through her. It sent an odd tremor through her nerves. 'No, I wasn't thinking that, as a matter of fact. I was just wondering.'

'I've just been having supper at your house,' he said, regarding her, and as casually as if he wasn't aware of interrupting her. 'With Tess, of course. How are you liking living in Dendaa? She seemed to think you were enjoying it.'

'Everyone's very friendly, thank you,' Kate said on a note of sudden wariness. So he had gone straight to see Tessa on his return—or perhaps she had known when he was coming, and invited him? That, somehow, annoyed her, so that she found herself saying, with careful formality to hide hostility, 'If you'll excuse me, Dr Kyle, it's time I want to check on Mrs Owani. She has a chest infection and I want to see how she's reacting to the antibiotic.'

'Then don't let me stop you. I'll do a wander round—which is, after all, what I came for in the first place.' He came to his feet as she did, so that for a moment they were standing close together. She felt, again, that overwhelming awareness of him which seemed for an instant menacing. And then, unexpectedly, he let out a chuckle, and as she looked up at him with surprise and a quick defensiveness, he said,

'You'll make a formidable ward sister one day—or maybe a matron? Why do I feel as if I've just stepped out of line, and been put in my place?'

'I—I don't know what you mean.'

'Yes you do. Or was your training hospital really as formal as that, and you're conditioned to it? Oh yes, of course, it was St John's, and that does have a name for being highly traditional.'

He was looking so amused that Kate bristled and leapt to the defence of her training without thinking twice about it. 'If you're trying to suggest St John's is old-fashioned—'

'Not in its treatments, I dare say—well I wouldn't dare say, when it has such a high reputation, and when Mutala seems to boast so many people who've worked there. But all this formality, even in the middle of the night! Now, where I trained, we'd have considered that very toffee-nosed! And I was thinking it was just *you*, Cousin Kate. But it isn't. You're not really so unfriendly after all, just proper!'

He was looking so mocking, and so entertained, that Kate felt a sudden urge to slap him. In the middle of a ward, too, just to wipe that outrageously appreciative expression off his handsome face and make him step back instead of looming over her with all that arrogant charm. It was lucky that the Unit door opened at that moment to bring the arrival of the two trainees back from lunch. It reminded Kate of where they were and gave her the chance to turn away with a flush crimsoning her cheeks and the sparkle of anger in her eyes. Even then, she was aware that Leah gave her an extremely curious look and was probably leaping to all the wrong conclusions, which was even more maddening than ever.

Kate swirled round with a crackle of her starched cotton skirt, in which the hospital laundry had overdone the stiffening again, and was suddenly extremely brisk and busy. And glad to feel Nick moving away to the opposite side of the ward after a tranquilly-murmured greeting to the trainees. How dare he sound so tranquil when he was so infuriating?

She kept to a different part of the Unit all the time he was in it, though when he had gone, after a casual wave in her direction across the dimness, she found that her anger had gone with him, leaving her feeling oddly flat. He hadn't said much, after all. It was just the way he had looked when he said it. And just when they had seemed to be getting on better, too. And, well, it was true that the St John's training was exceptionally formal, when other hospitals nowadays adopted a much more relaxed attitude. Kate knew, crossly, that she didn't like being made fun of just because she'd behaved automatically in the way she'd been trained to do.

She wrenched her mind away from him and was helped to forget him when she had to deliver the breech baby before the end of her shift. It was a difficult one, but not difficult enough to justify calling in a doctor, and since Sister had come on at eight they worked on it together. Kate went off duty feeling the glow which always came to her after a successful delivery which might have caused problems, and slept through the day remarkably dreamlessly until it was time to get up and go on duty again.

She arrived to find the Unit in a flurry because a set of instrumemts had gone missing, which was bad news indeed, considering they were short enough of them already. By the time those had been tracked down, a delivery was imminent, and then one of the prems developed hiccups. Kate coped, and was barely conscious of the passage of time. She was aware that it was midnight as she counted delivery packs and frowned over whether they would have enough. A moment later she was made aware that Nick was in the ward, because he appeared in the sluice doorway, murmured that he was merely doing a round, and then vanished again. She found herself wondering when he slept, but she certainly hadn't got time to sit around talking to him tonight.

Kate had quite forgotten that he had ever annoyed her by the time she saw him again, coming in answer to her call for a doctor in the early hours, when an emergency admission arrived in obstructed labour. He was just the person she most wanted to see, and she gave him a sympathetic smile when he arrived blinking, with his clothes obviously pulled on in a hurry.

'Sorry to wake you, but it didn't even seem worth taking her off the stretcher.' She found that she carefully didn't say, 'Dr Kyle,' this time. 'Everything's been at a dead stop for some time, apparently, and the foetal heartbeat's weakening.'

'Have you alerted theatre to switch everything on?' he asked, after a brief examination, and when she nodded, said, 'Good girl. You've buzzed whoever's on anaesthetic call, too? Right. Can you come in yourself?'

It was no worse than going on call-out and leaving a senior trainee in charge, and Kate nodded again, feeling unexpectedly pleased that he should want her. It would be the first time she had seen him operate, too. And somehow it wasn't surprising, a little time later, to see that he was quick and neat-fingered and could work fast without any sense of rush. As she stood carefully out of the way until the baby was freed and handed to her,

Kate found herself admiring his deftness, particularly when she considered that he had not been trained as a surgeon.

The reason for the obstructions became apparent as the baby showed itself in a tangle of cord. As soon as it was free Kate set to work with the resuscitator, to be rewarded after thankfully few seconds with a gasp and a yell. She saw Nick glance up, his eyes smiling above his mask, before he went back to concentrating on the mother. It gave Kate the comforting feeling of teamwork. It was almost as if he had said, again, 'Good girl,' and while she might have minded that from some people, or even thought it patronising, from him she wouldn't.

It was already getting light when they wheeled the unconscious mother back into the Unit. Kate had waited until the final stitching was done, staying in theatre to make a first examination of the baby and keeping the resuscitator handy in case of further problems. The baby girl seemed healthy enough now, though, with her heart-beat ticking steadily in its rapid rhythm and her eyes with their spiky lashes wide open in an unfocussed stare, which looked almost surprised to find herself born. Kate carried her through to make the statutory further check and weigh-in, and found that Nick had come to join her after seeing the mother transferred to a bed and already beginning to exchange an anaesthetised sleep for the lighter unconsciousness of ordinary slumber.

Kate found herself smiling at him. He was wearing his morning stubble again, giving him that raffish, pirat-ical air. His incipient beard was as fair as the bright tow-colour of his hair and stood out against his tan.

'Poor man, you're never off duty,' she said lightly. 'I saw from the records that you did a Caesar this after-noon, too!'

Nick's fingers, touching the tiny brown limbs of the baby Kate had just re-weighed, looked pale against the grape-bloom of the infant. He opened out the tiny palm for a careful test of the muscle-tension, showing the much paler skin.

'And a perfect little girl she is, too, isn't she? All of what—seven pounds? And no problems, apart from a fight with her own life-support. She can go in an ordinary crib, I think, not an incubator, thanks to your quick work with the resuscitator.'

'And yours in getting her free quickly. Just as well she doesn't need an incubator, since we haven't got a spare one at the moment.' Kate glanced at him quickly in case he thought it was a criticism of the hospital, but he seemed to be sharing her sense of pleasure at a job successfully done, because he merely smiled at her.

'Yes, better not to double up if we can avoid it. By the way, I noticed that you were trying to speak to the mother in her own language. You're coming on, aren't you?' he said idly.

'Not much,' Kate said ruefully, adding, 'I've been practising on other people as well as on the patients, and making them laugh with my accent! It's not the easiest language, is it? And there isn't even a dictionary.' She looked at him, her euphoria making her feel oddly relaxed. 'If there was, I'd have to keep asking how to say the words!'

'Easier just to learn it by sounds. I'm still stumbling over a lot of it.' He was looking at her with interest, so that she felt a sudden return of self-consciousness, aware of him directly opposite her with his hands spread out on the table between them. She reached quickly for a muslin nappy to wind expertly round the infant now that she had finished examining it, glad to have that to concentrate on. Nick went on standing there amiably. Perhaps he felt the need to unwind after the tension of operating, becacuse he went on talking instead of making a move to go.

'Going round the country helped me pick up quite a

lot, though you do run into some fairly impossible dialects! Have you managed to see much so far, or have you been sticking close to Mutala?'

'I've been down to Mafeking and out to the Dam, of course, though that's quite close. And to a couple of villages on call-out.' She kept her hands busy with the baby and added, for something to say, 'There isn't much to see, is there? Except scrub, and more scrub, and thorn trees! I haven't even seen any wild animals.'

'You won't, round here. But there is a designated wildlife area. I'll take you to see it, if you like.'

'I thought it was miles away?'

'Takes about two days to get there. There's a sort of primitive guest-house at Kolepou, for staying in, once you do get there. I'm owed some free days and I should imagine you could swop your duties around so as to add to yours, couldn't you?' he asked, raising an eyebrow at her.

Nothing could be more unexpected than such an invitation from him. Kate swallowed, feeling wary, startled, and confused. 'It—it depends what Tessa's doing,' she said hastily.

'You don't have to live in each other's pockets, do you? Anyway, she's already been up there a couple of times. They did one of their surveys in that direction.'

'Well, but—'

'There are all sorts of other things you've promised to do with your free time?' The grey eyes, which had been watching her with so much interest, blanked suddenly, and he said politely, 'It was just a cousinly suggestion. That baby's going to get cold if you leave it half-in and half-out of its nightie much longer!'

Kate bent her head quickly, feeling like flushing, her hands moving swiftly to tie the tapes on the cotton night-dress before lifting the baby against her shoulder with a feeling of defensiveness. By the time she looked up again he was stretching, preparing to move away, looking casual. Just as casual as if he was totally unaware of her shock and surprise, as if he hadn't really meant . . . Had he? That the two of them should go off alone together for several days? Well, if he had, it was only some kind of game he was playing with her, that was for sure, just to see how she would react.

It was almost unreal to hear him say, in perfectly normal tones,

'Time I went back to bed, I think! I've got an out patient clinic to start in two-and-a-half hours! I saw you checking up as we came in. There isn't anything else you want me to look at here, is there?'

'No.' There had been two normal births, with which the trainees had coped, and no panics. It was a relief to snap back into thinking about that, and push wariness and confusion away into the back of her mind. 'Nothing that need keep you,' she said, And, because it seemed suddenly important to sound as light and ordinary as he did, added, 'I will try not to wake you up again, I promise. That is, if you're going to get to sleep at all before you have to get up again!'

'Cat-napping is a way of life. I'll just take a quick look at this baby's mother on my way out, and then be off.' But he didn't move for a second. He glanced at Kate instead, and suddenly the amused, mocking expression was creeping back into his eyes. 'You know, you really are improving, and the way you're standing now suits you much better than all that prim folding-of-the-hands you were doing before.'

'It wouldn't be easy to fold my hands with a baby on my shoulder. And even our sister tutors didn't require us to stand looking correct when we were in the middle of something, even if we were supposed to do it whenever a senior doctor came round!' Kate retorted. She was going to answer back, even if she was going to refuse to be nettled by his teasing. Curiosity made her add, quickly, 'Where did *you* train, anyway?'

'Oh, somewhere very provincial by your standards!' Then he named the best-known hospital outside London with a glint in his eye. 'Good night, Cousin Kate,' he said, looking amused and rather obviously watching for her reaction. 'Or, I should say, good morning. No doubt I'll see you again tomorrow night, and we can discuss hospitals then, without your looking tempted to throw an infant at me!'

'Goodnight, Dr Kyle,' Kate said with deliberate decorum, just to annoy him, but feeling extraordinarily light of heart as he walked away chuckling. He was impossible, of course. Doubly impossible in the way he seemed to send her into a switchback of moods.

She shivered suddenly and moved swiftly to tuck the baby she was holding into its crib. No, he wasn't a comfortable person at all, however easy it had seemed, working with him tonight. He was too disturbing altogether, with that mocking smile which, all the same, seemed to have a quality of warmth in it, and that air of conscious masculine energy which seemed to radiate through the air. It wasn't difficult to remember that she had disliked him on sight for being much too handsome, with that firm jaw and straight nose and extraordinarily smoky grey eyes . . .

Which she had no intention of visualising, she decided rapidly, and particularly not when it meant she was standing here staring into space instead of getting back to work. What would Tessa have made of it if she had taken off into the bush for several days in Nick's company, as he had so casually suggested? Or of the remark that the two girls 'didn't have to live in each other's pockets'? Had she got it wrong about the situation between the two of them? Well, not, fairly obviously, on Tessa's side, but on his?

She found herself deciding, uncommonly crossly, that Tessa had probably told him he had got to show Kate more of Lanbwe, and he had certainly seemed relieved

when she refused. So there was no point in dwelling on
any of it. And it was a relief, and somehow a triumph,
to remember abruptly that she wouldn't be on duty
tonight anyway, because from nine a.m. she would start
her three days off.

Her three days off passed remarkably quickly, though
they did bring what she supposed was a message from
Richard when Tessa told her they would all meet up
at the university before the dance to hear the Vice-
Chancellor make a formal opening to the proceedings.
Richard was in Johannesburg, anyway, so he couldn't
have told her himself, though his absence didn't seem
to make Tessa any less busy.

Kate spent a lot of her time swimming in the Holiday
Inn pool, because although to a Lanbwena the weather
was comparitively cool, to her it was still right for
swimming and sunbathing, and chatting with the Dendaa wives who had taken to treating her as extended
family. She experimented with different ways of doing
her hair in a sudden fit of restlessness which, she told
herself firmly, had nothing to do with missing being at
work in the Unit. But when she went back, she felt
uncommonly glad to be there—back among the huts
and the walkways and the mothers and babies, so that
she could catch up on what had been going on in her
absence.

Nothing much had, except that there were different
faces in the beds and a couple of new trainees to replace
ones who had finished their qualifying spell. Sister was
back to saying, 'Call for Dr Kyle if you can, or Dr Kani
if not,' and if it was Nick who arrived, he gave Kate
only a brief, absent smile when they happened to pass
each other.

Kate was approaching the hospital for her second
day's afternoon duty when she felt a sudden slew of her
steering wheel, and an ominous bumping. A

puncture—and she was almost late arriving anyway. She pulled cautiously into the side of the road and jumped out to gaze in exasperation at a totally flat rear tyre. Well, since she was only just outside the hospital site, she would just have to leave it here and walk the rest of the way and mend it when she came off at seven. But it was annoying, even if it was the first trouble she had had with the small Volkswagen which was the same as Tessa's, only turquoise instead of orange.

She locked up carefully and glanced at the bungalows standing back from the road, hoping no one would mind a car apparently abandoned just outside them. Then she fled on duty, hurrying to take a short cut through the site, which was now familiar ground. She couldn't help wishing, a trifle guiltily, that the puncture had waited until she reached the hospital car park—because then she might have caught the eye of a friendly porter, and got some help with it.

Not that she couldn't change a wheel herself, she thought firmly some hours later. She hadn't even had a particularly hard afternoon on duty to give her the excuse for feeling discouraged. It was just a pity that so much Lanbwena dust seemed to have got on to the jack, so that her hands were filthy even before she'd properly started. Besides, she had to lie down in the edge of the road to discover where the points were.

She was groping to make sure she had found the right spot, amid the heavy layer of yellow dust which inevitably coated the car's underside, when she saw a pair of feet stop deliberately beside her. And then knees, as whoever it was squatted down beside her. She squinted up past the trousered legs, feeling thankful, if a little foolish, and then, almost with a feeling of inevitability, saw that she was looking up from this unfamiliar angle at a bronzed, firm-jawed face topped with tow-coloured hair.

'Not a new and original way of committing suicide, I

hope?' Nick asked mildly. 'Lie down and hope somebody starts the car and drives over you?'

'You can see perfectly well what I'm doing.' Kate
came upright, well aware that she must have a streak
of grime across her cheek, since she'd just absent-
mindedly rubbed it with one dirty hand, and gave him
a resentful glare. 'At least if you *can't* see that's a
puncture—'

'Yes, I saw it earlier. I recognised the car, too.' He
was eyeing her with a quite unnecessary amount of
amusement. 'I've been keeping an eye open for you out
of the window ever since I came off, as a matter of fact.
Or didn't you realise that you'd parked right outside
my house?'

'No, I didn't, I just stopped where it happened to
be!' The doctors' houses might well be just here, she
realized. She hadn't thought about it, though it did
explain how he did the sudden appearing act. And how
he came to be squatting here in casual slacks and shirt,
too, with his hair slightly wet and curling a little, as if
he'd just come out of the shower. Bitterly aware of the
contrast they must make, Kate found herself saying
sweetly, 'If you came out for a chat, do just sit there
while I get on.'

'No, I came out to offer to do it for you. But of
course, if you have such strong feminist principles that
you look on that as an insult . . .'

'No,' Kate said hastily, abandoning dignity in the face
of greater odds. She even found herself grinning at him
ruefully as she handed him the jack and moved out of
his way. She waited until he was safely occupied with
it, too, before adding, 'Not that I haven't changed
enough wheels in my time, mind! It's just that it isn't
my favourite job, not on a car I'm not actually used to.'

'What did you drive before?'

'A Mini. When I was doing Part Two, on the District,
it was the standard midwifery car. And always chose

two in the morning to have its punctures,' Kate said wryly. She watched Nick with a touch of chagrin as he undid the wheel nuts with an easy flick, when for her they always seemed to stick. She couldn't help noticing, too, how broad and well-shaped his hands were, and remembering she'd noticed that before. She went on quickly, trying to sound light to cover a feeling of awkwardness. 'There aren't many knight-errants around at two in the morning in Bow, either. It's very kind of you to—'

'Think nothing of it. I couldn't leave you languishing right on my doorstep, could I?' He answered her perfectly civilly, so there was no reason to imagine that he might have been going to add, 'Cousin Kate,' or to feel surprisingly disappointed because he didn't. His head was bent, examining the wheel he had just taken off. 'Looks as if you may have run over a thorn. Held for a little while and then went down suddenly, I should think, did it?'

'Yes. I think it was probably when I swerved off the road on my way in.' She gave him a defensive glance as he looked round at her with a swift frown. 'No, I wasn't being careless, it was just that this creature suddenly lumbered out across the road and gave me a shock. About six foot long and armoured, like a dragon.'

'Oh, an iguana. Yes, they do stray near town occasionally. You must have seen the smaller ones, though, surely?'

'Small ones are different,' Kate pointed out, remembering the shock the giant reptile had given her, though it had intrigued her, too. She had even sat for a moment to watch it lumbering off, fascinated by the spiky fan spread out behind the reptilian head.

'Mm. But I don't want to find myself patching you up in theatre after an accident. There you are, all done,' Nick said abruptly, before she could open her mouth to assure him that she did drive carefully. 'I'll give this to

Selandi in Maintenance and tell him it's for one of the nurses. That way he'll do it quickly so that you can have it back in the morning. Don't go out driving without a spare, except for coming back to the hospital.'

'Thank you, and yes, I do know!'

'All right, don't snap.' He raised an eyebrow at her, to her chagrin. 'You'd better come in and wash before you go home.'

She could hardly refuse. Besides, she was suddenly curious to see where he lived. She walked beside him up the short drive.

'Semi-detached. I've got this half and Lanji Jeriku and his wife have the other,' he said casually as he pushed open the front door which he had left ajar. 'Go through there and you'll find the bathroom. I'll go and wash in the kitchen.'

The bathroom was small and a little steamy, suggesting that Kate had been right about him being freshly out of the shower. There was a towelling bathrobe hanging on the back of the door. When she wiped the mirror clear and caught sight of her own appearance, it was grubby enough to make her reach hastily for the sponge lying on the basin. Then she had to rinse the sponge thoroughly because she seemed to have filled it with grit off her hands, and she was self-consciously aware of being a long time as she hurriedly tried to do something about the way her hair had started coming loose.

She came out of the bathroom as quickly as she could, resisting the temptation to look round curiously, and hesitated in the small hallway. Should she just go? Then his voice called out, 'Kate? In here.'

She walked into a room which seemed pleasantly furnished, if with the standard government furniture, and was obviously the sitting-room. He was standing in the middle of it and it felt suddenly small with him standing there among his possessions.

'Want a cold drink? Squash or lime juice? I'm having one. I won't offer you alcohol when you're straight off duty and driving!'

'I—I'd better go, thank you.'

'Sure?' He gave her such a curious look that she had to glance away from him. Since her eye immediately fell on an African mask it was hardly surprising that he said, 'Admiring the African head, or hating it? Oh, Tessa's got a similar one, so you must be used to living with it!'

'I don't think it's quite the same.' To lighten things, and to feel that she hadn't stiffened into self-consciousness, Kate made herself gaze deliberately round the room. Anywhere but at him.

Suddenly her eyes were caught by something. The rest of the room seemed to go into a bright blur around her. A family photograph, a group of about a dozen people, smiling at the camera and looking cheerful, obviously in their best clothes. And one face in particular seeming to leap out at her. It was almost like looking in the mirror, except that it was a masculine face instead of a feminine one. And older. And like looking down a long tunnel into the past.

She heard Nick's voice behind her say swiftly, 'I'm sorry, I'd forgotten that was there,' but she had already turned away in a sharp gesture. She met his eyes with a sudden blankness, unconscious of him for a second except as someone tall and solid and standing in her way. He said again, 'I'm sorry, I genuinely didn't do that on purpose, you know.' And then, quite gently and without any of his usual mockery, 'Go on, look at it. You obviously want to.'

'No, not particularly. I just—it just—'

By way of answer he reached past her and picked up the photograph, holding it out to her. Kate *didn't* want to look at it—it aroused a sharp pain of repudiation, even if that was mingling with a wistful curiosity which she certainly didn't want to feel. When something else slipped out from behind the cardboard frame and fell to the floor, she bent down swiftly, glad to have something to distract her.

It was another photograph, a smaller one, but it didn't represent the danger of the first. It was simply a head and shoulder portrait of an exceptionally pretty girl with short red hair, smiling into the camera. She found herself studying it intently for somewhere to look, until Nick's other hand came out and took it away from her, firmly.

'No, not that one.' His voice was suddenly dry, making her stiffen into defensiveness. 'I wondered where I'd put that.'

'Why, who is it? Oh, Dr Harvey?' Kate asked, remembering, feeling suddenly sure that the red-haired beauty must be the same girl whose round, perfect handwriting she had spent such hours sorting through.

'Gina? No, she was a Californian blonde. This one had a rather different history,' he said, and reached out abruptly to open a drawer, thrust the photograph in it, and shut it again. 'Stop changing the subject in that deliberate way, Kate,' he said, with enough command in his voice to make her jump. 'And stop pretending you don't suffer from normal curiosity, too! Yes, that *is* your father—taken about eighteen months ago at a family wedding. It's most of the Kyle clan, in fact, which is why I've got it out on display, to remind me of home. Want to know who everybody is?'

He obviously intended to tell her and she did want to know, somehow, particularly when he put it like that. Even if . . .

She lowered her eyes to the photograph, even let him put it in her hand, and followed his pointing finger with a feeling of numb obedience.

'My parents,' he said, 'and those are my two sisters. That one's my elder sister's husband, and that's their toddler. That Janna, my brother's fiancée, but he's not in it because he's taking the photo. That's Norma, just there.'

He paused, as if making sure she really looked at 'that woman', who was dark-haired and pleasant-faced and had a smile which, involuntarily, reminded her of Nick's own. 'And there on the end, of course, is David, your father.'

'Thank you, but I do recognise him. Did you think I wouldn't?' Kate asked in a hostile voice. But not quite as hostile as she had meant it to come out. There was an unwary edge of longing in it too, because it wasn't really possible not to feel a stir of emotion as she looked down at the remembered face. She hadn't got a photograph of him anywhere near as recent as this, to show her how he had looked before he died.

Almost as if he was reading her mind, Nick said, 'I could get you a copy of this if you like. Just him I mean, taken off the end and enlarged. I know someone among the mine advisers with a photo lab, and I'm sure it's possible.'

'No, thanks!' She had thrust the photograph back at him abruptly. 'No thanks,' she said again, stiffly. 'It really isn't necessary to bother your friend. After all, why should I want—'

'Forgive me for thinking you might be human.' The sardonic note was back in his voice in full force, as he added, 'And forgive me for the fact that you had me fooled for a moment.' He turned away, moving to put the photograph down flat on a desk at the far side of the room, and speaking over his shoulder with a cool sarcasm. 'No, of course, you don't want a photograph of him, do you? Not even to remember him by! And why should anyone care, since he isn't here any more to talk about you? Or to sound wistful about his only daughter? Though I must say, I never knew him when he wasn't carrying a picture of *you*—even one he'd had specially sent to him by your local paper, after you'd won some prize or other at the end of your first year of nursing.'

He still had his back to her. He turned round too soon. Then he was across the room in quick strides and his arms were going round her in a warm embrace as she gulped and tried to stop the tears running down her cheeks with desperate fingers.

'Idiot,' he said above her head, but sounding as if he meant it for himself, not her. And then, gently, 'Jealousy is a killer, isn't it? Mike and John weren't all his life, you know.'

'I—I didn't know!'

'Idiot,' he said again, and this time he obviously did mean it for her. She felt his lips brush her forehead. 'Why d'you think I'd heard so much about you that I could recognise you on sight? I've probably heard your name mentioned more often than—Want a handkerchief?'

'I'm all right. I'm—I'm *perfectly* all right.' It was a great deal too much, suddenly to be standing so close to him, close in the circle of his arms, feeling his strength. Kate pushed herself away from him, scrabbling in her pocket for a handkerchief of her own, scrubbing her face with it, putting a space between them. She didn't seem to have any dignity left, against the shaken feeling which was catching at her, but she tried to collect some. 'If—if I could just go back in to your bathroom and wash my face again?'

'Be my guest. But if you're in there too long I shall come in after you, to make sure you are all right.'

'I am. Honestly. And I don't want—I don't want to talk about it.'

'OK,' he said peaceably. His eyes were filled with a rueful understanding, and extraordinarily gentle. Kate escaped because she had to, or else be drawn back to him again—back to that magnetism of his which she could feel even at this moment.

She splashed her face with cold water and scrubbed her cheeks with a towel which was still damp, until they flamed. Her reflection in the mirror looked strange, bright-eyed and tremulous, like somebody completely different. Nothing like the cool, controlled Kate Raven at all. She felt as if she had been pulled apart and not quite put back together again. And what on earth were they going to say to each other when she went back into the other room?

She was hesitating when her eye was caught by something on the floor. It was lying as if it had been dropped and had landed in a corner. Kate bent to pick it up and found herself holding a girl's bracelet. An unusual one, made from linked strips of copper alternating with the polished striped stones she knew were called tiger's eyes because she had seen them in the local shops. A girl's bracelet in Nick's bathroom?

She found herself steady suddenly, and cold, and remembering all sorts of things. He was a handsome, footloose bachelor. He could be extraordinarily kind; well, she had known that from the way he could gentle nervous patients. But it was an impersonal kindness. He could even extend it to a stray cousin if she happened to get upset.

And poor Tessa! There she was, caught up in a state of obvious fascination with the man—and even if he went to supper with her occasionally, and treated her to doses of his undoubted charm, he also kept a photograph of some red-headed girl in his house and had odd bracelets scattered about. Someone had, presumably, taken off the bracelet for a bath or a shower or, she thought with sudden heavy sarcasm, for some other even more intimate occupation . . .

She put the bracelet carefully on the shelf over the basin where it could be seen, and swept out of the bathroom with something like her customary staff nurse's tread. In spite of all her attempts, something must have been showing in her face as she paused in the sitting-room doorway, because Nick's head tilted to one side abruptly in a quizzical expression. If it made Kate's heart give one unwary thump before it settled down like a cold stone in her stomach, she tried to ignore it.

'Better? Now don't go back into the deep-freeze, Cousin Kate, because I was just about to suggest you stayed and had something to eat with me,' he said.

He had no right to give her that charming smile, which seemed to turn her knees to water. 'Thank you,' Kate said, smiling back at him and trying very hard not to look frosty, 'but I really must get home. And thank you for changing my wheel for me.'

'All right, then. Don't drive into any iguanas and remember you haven't got a spare wheel until tomorrow.'

He walked across the room. Kate tried to still her inclination to back. But it was all right to move away from him, because he was coming to show her out of the front door. He even stepped out into the drive with her and accompanied her back to where the small turquoise Volkswagen squatted at the kerb. Kate climbed quickly into it and leaned across to give him a smile which seemed to stretch her muscles in an artificial fashion.

'Thanks again. I hope—I hope you have a nice peaceful evening, and don't get called in for once!'

'Not supposed to be my shift,' he said, smiling back at her. 'Take care. See you tomorrow.'

She drove away, wanting to watch in the mirror to see if he stood there until she had gone. But when she did, he wasn't visible. He must have turned away at once and gone inside. She knew it shouldn't matter.

Just because she had fallen apart suddenly and cried all over him, just because he had put his arms around her—

She was in love with *Richard*. She'd been in love with Richard for years. But the thought of Richard didn't bring its customary balm. In fact it left her with a completely blank feeling.

CHAPTER SIX

THERE WAS one advantage of a highly formal hospital training: it gave perfect practice in not showing one's feelings.

So it was possible to give Nick a coolly pleasant smile when he appeared in the Unit next day, though Kate was glad she had the excuse of a patient calling out to her so that she could walk away from him on legs which suddenly seemed to turn to cotton wool.

When it was time for her to go to lunch in the canteen, which was used by all the staff, she carefully didn't go. She went to pick up her spare wheel from Selandi instead, finding it ready for her as promised, and then drove quickly into Mutala to replace lunch with some of the overpriced fruit on sale, which she didn't feel at all like eating.

She wasn't in love with Nick, of course. It was just a temporary madness. An infection—like catching flu. It would go away if she didn't think about it. Anyway, she certainly wasn't going to show it, even by the faintest flicker a resentment which, fortunately, he would only misunderstand. In fact she wasn't going to show anything at all.

She *had* to run into him on the walkways on her way off duty. He was standing still, looking idle for once, but since he saw her before she saw him, she couldn't turn off and take another route.

'Get your wheel back all right?' he asked.

'Oh, yes, thanks.'

'Good. By the way—'

What he would have said then, with that friendly, slightly quizzical smile, remained unspoken, because a staff nurse put her head out of the nearest hut doorway and called to him. He spared Kate a rueful grin and turned away. And she walked on, filled with the confusion of knowing, somehow, that he had been waiting for her, deliberately standing there when he knew she was due off duty. Of course it wasn't that at all . . . Unless, of course, he'd been standing there out of a kindly inclination to keep an eye on her. He might just do that, after the incredibly stupid way she'd cried all over him yesterday.

She didn't want to dwell on the extraordinary mixture of qualities which characterised him. She'd spent enough time doing that last night, with a mixture of anger and confusion and yearning and, occasionally, despair. For goodness' sake, she didn't even like him, most of the time. But liking, a whisper inside her head retorted, had nothing to do with his capacity to dazzle her with his smile, or churn her up with his mockery, or make her tremble at the memory of an embrace which, to him, had merely been a gesture of automatic kindness.

She drove back to Dendaa savagely reminding herself that Nick had enough girls already on his string. And she had been quite happy before, and no doubt would be again. It wouldn't be long before he did or said something so outrageous that she could hate him outright, anyway. Oh yes, she would certainly get over it.

As she had got over Richard.

She was still going to the dance with Richard, who seemed such a stranger that she couldn't imagine what they would have to say to each other during an entire evening. After that, it didn't help to get home to find Tessa there, gloomily surveying a crumpled Laura Ashley dress and saying that since it was the only formal garment she owned, she supposed she'd have to wear it. She glanced up at Kate, adding, 'Not that I'll look like much in it. And I hate dressing up.'

'Nonsense, you'll look very pretty in it. Is,' Kate's voice was light, 'Nick coming to the dance?'

'Yes,' Tessa said, looking suddenly more cheerful. 'He's fixed it so that he can get away. He said he couldn't let anything *that* important pass without his putting in an appearance.'

She didn't seem to notice that Kate had raised Nick's name first, for once. Then she changed the subject abruptly to talk about the difficulties one of their neighbours had been having with a gardener, so that Kate couldn't go on talking about the dance, or improvise hastily that she wasn't sure, after all, whether she might have to stay on duty. But she couldn't really say that anyway, when it could too easily be found out to be a lie.

Perhaps she had tempted providence, because she *was* late off duty on the night of the dance. Very late. There had been a premature delivery, and then two other normal deliveries, then the prem baby to keep an eye on, and then a panic because they were running out of delivery packs and a couple more mothers were imminent. Sister was off duty too, and there was too much for too few trained pairs of hands to do. Kate came off feeling rushed and wishing that the changeover shift between day-staff and night-staff, which was supposed to be a short one and left to the senior trainees, hadn't brought so many problems tonight of all nights.

At least she wasn't keeping Tessa waiting, because Tessa had said she had to go early anyway, and help with the arrangements, but it seemed so awful to be thoroughly and rudely late that she felt like not turning up at all.

Nevertheless, she wriggled into the dress she had bought a week ago. There had been nothing in her trunk either good enough or formal enough to wear in this country where, apparently, evening dress was always worn long, and she tried not to feel a tremor of nervousness, confusion and anger as she regarded herself in the mirror. The dress was a South African import from a Mutala boutique and she had chosen it in deliberate contrast to the neat severity of her nurse's uniform. It was flame-coloured silk chiffon with a closely-moulded bodice, tiny straps across the shoulders, and a full, swirling skirt. She knew the vivid colour went well against the tan which was now lending a glow to her fair skin and giving the blue of her eyes an unusual depth. She had planned to pile her hair up on top of her head in a new and more elaborate style to go with the elegance of the dress, but now that she was so late there wasn't time for that. She began to coil it into its usual bun. Then, in a fit of defiance, she simply brushed it out and left it loose. The slim but curvy figure in the flame-coloured dress, with a sheet of shimmering fairness framing her face and swirling down past her bare shoulders, looked like somebody else entirely. Almost unrecognisable.

She told herself it was only that—and her lateness, of course—which made her arrive at the university feeling nervous, but trying to hide it behind a studied calm.

Everything, fairly obviously, was in full swing. Walking into the long, high hall and hesitating, Kate was aware of a lot of people dancing to the music which seemed to echo a little from the corners of the ceiling. There didn't seem to be many of the Lanbwena students there, though there were expatriate teenagers who had probably come with their parents.

Tables had been set around the edges of the room with a long buffet laid out at one end. A large and complicated tape-recorder at the other end was providing the music. Tessa wasn't immediately evident, though Kate caught sight of two Dendaa couples among the dancers and received friendly waves and cheerfully appreciative looks. She looked round quickly for Richard—and then saw him, sitting at one of the tables in conversation with a middle-aged African.

It was like looking at a stranger. That blank feeling came back, the sense of looking at a man she didn't know and never had known. But that was nonsense. Kate stilled her inclination to laugh hysterically and threaded her way firmly round the dancers towards Richard's table, taking a sudden extreme care not to look anywhere else but where she was going. And then, because he was talking, she had to hesitate self-consciously beside the table, caught up in the suddenly embarrassing knowledge that she had dressed to look different for him—but the result might be that he wouldn't recognise her.

He didn't for a moment. He glanced up politely to give her a vague smile. And then looked more closely and said, 'Kate!' on such a note of surprise that she felt more self-conscious than ever. He was wearing a light-weight grey suit which seemed to hang on his lanky frame a little as he got up to pull a chair out for her, and he and the African with him were wearing ties, though most of the expatriate men seemed to have decided to go without that formality.

'I'm terribly sorry to be so late. I'm afraid I got held up on duty.'

'I'm sure you can be forgiven. I'm not sure where Tessa's got to,' he said ruefully, looking around. 'She was here a moment ago. Oh, do you know Dr Anji, Dean of the new medical school?'

Kate received a formal handshake from the Lanbwena doctor and they all sat down again. She began to murmur a further apology for being late, but Dr Anji was asking her politely how long she had been in Lanbwe and whether she was enjoying her work at the hospital. Kate found herself being reminded of Matron when he said that Mutala Nurses' Training

School would soon be producing a full quota of home-grown nurses, though he was too civil to say it with the pointedness which that lady would undoubtedly have put into it! Unfortunately, the memory also reminded her of Nick. She concentrated quickly on what Dr Anji was saying, deciding that she wasn't going to look round to see where Nick was . . .

And then Richard was offering to fetch her something to eat and drink. She refused the food, but agreed shyly that she would like a glass of fruit juice because that seemed to be what he was drinking. In a moment she would stop feeling unreal, of course she would, and get him back into focus. But she wished she didn't feel as if her tongue had cloven to the roof of her mouth as he came back with a glass for her and sat listening to her continued stilted conversation with Dr Anji.

It was a relief when the music came to a pause and the dancers came wandering off the floor, because Kate, who had carefully not been looking at them but had kept her eyes on Dr Anji's face in a way which she was sure he must find unnaturally polite, had the distraction of being introduced to several other people who came to sit down with them.

There was an elderly Dutchman who was apparently a visiting Professor of Mathematics, and there was Mrs Anji, who was quite young, and pregnant enough for Kate to wonder, with a further bubble of hysteria, whether her services might be called on before the end of the evening. And there were another couple whose names Kate didn't catch. They were middle-aged again, and with accents which didn't sound quite Lanbwena. A moment later Tessa arrived, brought back to the table by one of their Dendaa friends who gave Kate a grin and then went away again. Tessa sat down beside Kate. She was looking unusually pretty with a tinge of pink in her cheeks, and the fine sprigged cotton which out-lined her small bust and then fell to her feet from a gathering of tiny pleats suited her, though Kate wished she could have left off her glasses which half hid the big, pansy-brown eyes.

'You did make it all right, then.' The look she was giving Kate seemed oddly defensive. 'I was beginning to think I ought to come back and look for you!'

'Sorry, we had a dreadfully busy day. Or evening. It was—'

'You haven't missed much, actually. Only the Vice-Chancellor making a speech of welcome and starting everything off. That's him and Mrs Hariku over there, doing the rounds. I think they're leaving after that. Nick,' she said casually, 'hasn't got here yet either, so I thought you were probably tied up in some crisis or other.'

'We didn't call him in. I don't know what he's—'

At that moment Dr Anji asked her politely if she would like to dance, as the music started up again. The elderly Dutch Professor promptly asked Tessa. The other couple got up again and Richard stayed at the table talking to Mrs Anji, who was fanning herself in an animated fashion.

Kate knew it was just as well to be dancing, before Tessa could notice that she had suddenly sounded snappish. She knew, too, that she could stop carefully *not* looking round at the dancing couples for the sight of one particular fair head amongst them.

As she made further stilted conversation with Dr Anji, whose style on the dance-floor definitely owed more to *Come Dancing* than to disco, she tried not to feel stifled. She tried guiltily not to feel that it would have been more pleasant to have come to the dance in the company of the Sinclairs or the Barkers or the Rouses, all of whom had suggested she joined up with them before she had said she was coming with the university party.

But she had come to see Richard, she reminded

herself quickly, and when Peter Sinclair appeared beside her just as Dr Anji was leading her back to the table, she smilingly refused to dance any more at the moment, even though the foot-tapping number which was just starting made her feel faintly wistful. Peter gave her a grin and said he would definitely be back to claim her later, adding with friendly admiration that when she was looking so gorgeous, she wouldn't be allowed to claim 'nurse's feet' for the entire evening.

Kate grinned back at him and then found herself explaining carefully to Dr Anji that Peter was her next-door neighbour. She didn't know why she was bothering really, except to be polite. But Dr Anji seemed so formal that he might have taken the apparent flirtatiousness in Peter's manner for something more than it was, when actually he was only being his normal friendly self.

She might have mistaken it too, in the old days . . .

She sat down beside Richard, feeling muddled suddenly, and as if she had been given a vision of a prim and studious Kate which filled her with embarrassment. And then she had to try to look intelligent because everybody seemed to be exchanging serious comments about the political situation in different African countries.

The Dutch Professor seemed to have visited several of them, as had Richard, of course. The conversation threaded its way through the disco beat in the background and ignored it, as if this was a seminar rather than a social event.

All around the rest of the room people were dancing and drinking and laughing. And Nick still wasn't here, Kate thought, knowing that she had just taken an involuntary glance round to look for him. A fair head at the far end of the room had made her heart lurch suddenly, but it hadn't been him after all. It was all wrong to feel so drained and flat and pointlessly dressed up, just because he wasn't here.

He was. Kate was suddenly all too aware of it as she

realised that he was only six feet away from her and standing beside Tessa's chair at the end of this very table. He must have just arrived, looking neat and tidy and somehow well-scrubbed, in a dark green shirt which set off his fairness and contrasted with off-white linen trousers and a matching jacket slung casually over one shoulder. He was bending over Tessa to murmur something with a smile, while she looked up at him in welcome. And then, before Kate could drag her eyes away, he had drawn one hand from his pocket to give Tessa something—was lifting her wrist to help her fasten it. A bracelet, showing up clearly in a glint of copper and small shiny stones . . .

It was just as well that the teenage son of one of the Dendaa families was suddenly drawing her attention by standing in front of her, shyly asking if she'd like to dance. Since he was only thirteen, and looking as if he had plucked up courage to ask her, she certainly couldn't refuse—in fact she was on her feet at once. Then a remembered politeness made her turn to Richard, touching his sleeve to gain his attention, saying as his head came round towards her, 'Would you mind if I . . .?'

'No, of course. Do go and enjoy yourself!'

He said it so much like an uncle that Kate felt a wild desire to laugh. It was a relief to be moving away on to the dance-floor instead of sitting there in a state of numb shock—certainly a shock she shouldn't have been feeling. Considering the way Tessa felt about Nick, it was just as well if he wasn't carrying on with someone else. Just as well that the bracelet Kate had last seen in Nick's bathroom had turned out to be hers, after all. Just as well, even if . . .

The only thing to do was to look happy and sociable, so Kate did. She even gave her young partner a conspiratorial grin when they were far enough from the table, and whispered a thank-you for rescuing her from a

boring conversation. That made him relax and look less
agonisingly solemn, which was all to the good. And she
would *not* look round to see where Nick, now, would
be dancing with Tessa.

Since Richard hadn't sounded at all as if he minded
parting with her, in fact had told her to go and enjoy
herself, she went to have a drink with young Dominic's
parents after their dance. And then danced with one or
two other people who came up and asked her with
flattering promptness as soon as she was free.

Then Peter Sinclair appeared in front of her, telling
her that it was his turn, and besides, his wife had gone
off with an agriculturalist so he was perfectly entitled to
take refuge in asking the next most beautiful girl in the
room to dance with him. Kate parried his deliberately
extravagant compliments and exchanged laughter with
Penny Sinclair when they danced up close to her and
she leaned over to assure Kate that her husband had
only been waiting for a chance to grab her because he'd
always preferred blondes.

Then she had to try to copy some of James Barker's
extremely nimble footwork, and then more of the same
with David Rouse as the tape-recorder produced an
increasingly disco type of beat. She seemed to be smiling
and laughing until her face ached, and if she was aware,
more than once, of not quite catching Nick's eye, it was
perfectly easy to turn her shoulder every time she saw
him and look firmly in some other direction.

He didn't seem to be dancing with Tessa all the time.
In fact she saw him at least twice with a brunette of
about Kate's own age, who was very thin and wearing
a striking dress which struck Kate as being much too
low-cut for anyone who had so little bosom, making her
look skinny instead of flattering her. Not that she cared
who he danced with. At last she joined up with the
Barkers to go and sample the food laid out on the buffet.

The food was standard party snacks, chicken and

salad and rolls filled with prawns, but Kate couldn't help remembering, guiltily, that everything visible, except perhaps the chicken, must have been imported. Perhaps it was that, or conscience, which drove her to claim a temporary tiredness and walk deliberately back to the table where Richard was still sitting.

He was alone, too, which made here feel guilty all over again. Not that he looked as if he minded; in fact he looked round with an abstracted air when Kate sat down beside him. He smiled at her, but went back to gazing apparently unseeingly at the dance-floor with a slight frown between his brows. He didn't seem to have missed her or to feel inclined to talk to her either.

Kate tried to think of something to say to him and found her mind instantly empty. Had she ever known what his interests were, besides work? Had she ever known anything about him at all? She looked away from him quickly, feeling uncomfortable, and shook her hair back over her shoulders in a sharp gesture. There was a touch of desperation in thinking that he might at least ask her to dance. She *was* here at his invitation—even if she'd hardly been near him all evening . . .

She still couldn't think of anything to say, but when she cleared her throat involuntarily it seemed to wake him up and he snapped to attention to give her his familiar sweet smile.

'I've got two left feet, I'm afraid,' he said apologetically. 'It does give me the perfect excuse not to take part, but I feel as if you're definitely being wasted.'

'No, of course not,' Kate disclaimed hastily. He hadn't, now she came to think of it, danced with anyone. She glanced involuntarily towards the dance-floor and saw, as if her eyes were instantly drawn there, Tessa and Nick dancing together to a slow number. And saying something to each other which looked uncommonly serious. She returned her attention to Richard quickly, and asked, 'How's—how's work going?'

'Little by little, as usual,' he said pleasantly.

'Kwashiorkor's an odd word,' Kate said unthinkingly, and then flushed. 'I'm sorry, that probably sounds very ignorant!'

'No, why should you know? It's actually a West African word meaning "the superseded one". When a mother has a second child, the first gets put on to a mixture of corn and water instead of milk. I expect you were wondering why you hadn't seen the "kwashiorkor look" anywhere among your new babies, but of course it doesn't happen until later.'

'Oh, I—I see.' It was very interesting, even if it was hardly party conversation. 'How many countries have you actually been to in the last two years?' she asked gravely.

'Six or seven. We did a lot of travelling in the beginning. Mainly in the more primitive areas, away from the cities.' He was answering her with his usual politeness when Tessa appeared abruptly in front of them, and he broke off, smiled at her, and said, 'Oh, there you are!'

Here was Nick, too. Kate had already been aware of it. What she hadn't expexted was that he would reach down and pull her to her feet, and as soon as he touched her she felt so completely boneless that she couldn't have resisted.

'I'm stealing Kate,' he said cheerfully to Richard, 'since it's the first time she's kept still enough for me to catch her and make her dance with me!' And with that he had left Tessa beside Richard, and was moving Kate back on to the floor.

He was looking much too handsome, lit up with an easy charm, holding her close against him with a loose, relaxed grasp, and moving to the slow dance with the energy which characterised him muted into a kind of languor. Kate found her steps fitting his and she felt a ridiculous inclination to relax dreamily against his broad shoulder.

'You seem to have been making hay with a lot of husbands, and causing a lot of wives to mutter cattily that they might think of bleaching their hair!' he said amiably.

His voice showed that he was teasing. Kate found that she wasn't in any mood to be teased. She couldn't think of an immediate retort to make, only an urgent desire to keep the conversation as light as possible. He must know perfectly well that her hair was natural.

She wanted, oh how she wanted, to be completely indifferent to him. Not to be aware that dancing with him made her feel as if she was melting inside. Perhaps the lager she'd been drinking was stronger than she realised. After all the control she had been exerting over herself, it must be only that—

He didn't seem cast down by her silence. 'How silky your hair is,' he murmured, running one finger down the blonde tresses against her shoulder. 'You should let it loose more often.'

'Oh, sure,' Kate found her voice. 'It would be very suitable for ward work, wouldn't it!'

'It'd certainly brighten things up—but I suppose it would rather get in your way!'

'Tessa—' Kate began, with a feeling of determination, but he finished the sentence for her.

'Is looking very sweet too. But *you're* looking extraordinarily beautiful. I'm sure I'm not the first person to say that tonight, but I'm entitled to be repetitive, aren't I?'

Half of her wanted to snap, 'Don't practise your charm on me,' but the other half, unwarily, felt a glow from the compliment. And she seemed to be mesmerised by the desire to drift even closer against him and enjoy the sensation of being held against that hard muscularity.

Kate made herself look up into his eyes, the sparkle in her own coming from a mixture of uncertainty and anger. How easy it would be to forget everything now that she was with him. 'I'm just the same Staff Nurse Raven you see every day,' she said.

'No way. We'd have every male for miles around beating a path to the door of Maternity.' The look he was giving her now was more thoughtful than teasing, with a smoky flame in the grey eyes which gave her a tingle of shock and made her look away quickly. She heard Nick murmur, 'You know, little cousin, Africa really does suit you.'

'Does it? One can get a tan in England too, you know.' It was impossible of him to say 'little cousin' on that caressing note. She hoped she was managing not to sound defensive, but suddenly she found a distraction, and went on, in her sweetest voice, 'Who's that dark girl in the zig-zag patterned dress, who looks as if she's had a bit much to drink? Oh, sorry, she's a friend of yours, isn't she? I don't think I've seen her before.'

'She's the wife of the South African geological adviser up at Williamstown. They're down for the dance, and I know them because they put me up while I was there. They're called George and Sarah Shultz, and I can introduce you if you like—though they're going back tomorrow.'

His casual answer shouldn't have annoyed her, but somehow it did. Or perhaps the prickle of discomfort she felt came from the way his hand had moved round under her hair and was idly caressing the bare skin above the low back of her dress. Just as if it was an automatic gesture to stroke the nearest female. Kate tried to move a little away from him, feeling suddenly inclined to ask snappishly why the red-haired girl wasn't here. And whether Tessa was glad to get her bracelet back, too.

'It's nice of you to offer me a duty-dance, when you have to share yourself around so much,' she said instead.

'Don't be spiky. It doesn't suit you when you're

looking so much softer than usual. You're as prickly as a cactus—or a thorn tree!'

He was smiling, the grey eyes, so close above hers, looking down at her with that same smoky light in them. There was a silky quality which he could put into the deep tones of his voice, and he was doing it now, deliberately. It was just as if he had pulled her deliberately closer, too, or was that just to avoid a couple who, against the dreaminess of the music, had suddenly decided to do an elaborate and old-fashioned ballroom glide?

'Oh, oh look!' Kate said abruptly. As they turned, her eyes had caught the table she had just left. Richard was on his feet, and from the way he was ushering other people in front of him, was plainly planning to leave. And Tessa, unbelievably, seemed to be going with him. 'The party's breaking up,' Kate said breathlessly, 'We ought to—'

'It's only Richard, taking off with relief after doing his duty by being here. He isn't very sociable,' Nick said coolly.

'But—'

'But nothing.' Nick's arms had tightened just a little. It was plain that he didn't intend to interrupt their dance. 'I expect they're going off to have coffee in Richard's rooms. That doesn't mean you have to go. If you were wanted, I don't doubt Richard would have come across and fetched you! They're only going to have one of their interminable discussions, I expect.'

In which Kate would only feel like an outsider. And she didn't want to go—would be only too glad of the excuse not to. If that seemed incredible, in the face of all her past hopes and dreams, she could only acknowledge it wryly and then remember, clearly and coldly, that she had another reason for objecting. One which would surely show Nick how indifferent she was to dancing with him.

'I was wondering if you'd noticed,' she said rapidly, 'that he seems to be taking Tessa with him!'

'Why not, if she wants to go? I don't suppose she has any choice about the matter, anyway. Richard's the world's greatest manipulator when he wants something—and if he wants her to make the coffee, no doubt she will!' While Kate was still gasping over that, she felt a sudden hardening of his muscles to make her aware that his grip had become forceful rather than firm. 'No, you're not going to run after them,' he said on an abruptly icy note which brought her startled gaze back to his face to see, all at once, an angry jut to that determined jawline. 'You know, I did suspect, one afternoon a few weeks ago, that you were gazing rather adoringly at a certain person,' he said with heavy sarcasm. 'But I dismissed it, on the grounds that you obviously hardly knew the man anyway, and certainly hadn't seen him for two years.'

'I—I don't know what you mean!'

'Well, you do seem to be making rather heavy objections to his leaving without you, don't you? Is there a secret lurking under that prim and proper exterior, I wonder? A case of adolescent hero-worship, perhaps?'

The scorn in his voice was cutting, and all his old sardonic arrogance was back in the lift of his eyebrows and the curl of his mouth, and in the hardness which had come into the grey eyes, making them look like ice-chips. Kate was both bewildered and furious. How did he dare? And she had only been thinking of Tessa anyway, determinedly, virtuously; thinking that Tessa was being dragged away from Nick. And that he might mind. And, all at once, he didn't seem to, so that she felt as scornful as he looked. *Womaniser!* She certainly wasn't going to give her friend away, though, or give the least hint that she knew how Tessa felt about him. That would be adding insult to injury.

'I certainly admire Professor Cranshaw,' she said

coolly, with a shake in her voice, barely noticing that she had given him his title instead of referring to him as Richard. 'Who wouldn't? Apart from being brilliant and dedicated, he's a very civilised man!'

'Really? So there *is* something in it! Well, well.' He was looking down at her with a sharp mockery. 'A good staff midwife you may be, and I'll have to admit you are, but you're still determined to keep away from reality in your private life, aren't you? Love-at-a-distance—so much safer!'

'Is this a private fight, or can anyone join in?'

They were still dancing, or rather standing still in the middle of the floor, and the interruption, delivered with a bright laugh, came from the thin girl Kate had noticed earlier. She surged up beside them in a partner's arms, her bright green eyes flashing with a slightly tipsy amusement. She definitely was drunk, Kate thought with distaste—and her husband, if that was him, seemed cheerfully unembarrassed by the fact. Nick's mouth closed with a snap, but he didn't let go of Kate as she'd hoped he might. He went on holding her in that inescapable grip, and managed to produce a grim smile.

'Yes, Sarah, it *is* a private fight, as a matter of fact. This is Kate, a distant relative of mine with an unfortunately quarrelsome nature. And since she's in one of her moods, I'm going to take her outside and let her finish spitting at me there!'

'Go on and give it to him, girlie,' the husband said with a leer, which made Kate even more furious than ever, and danced his wife away, against her quite audible protest. Nick, looking down with a brief hard-eyed stare accompanied by a glittering smile for everyone else's benefit, kept Kate clamped to his side as he walked her rapidly off the dance-floor.

Outside it was dark, and the chill in the air made Kate give a sudden shiver. Nick manhandled her across the open space until they came into the lee of a building, his arm round her shoulders looking, to anyone who might see them, Kate supposed, like an affectionate gesture designed to keep her warm. Only she knew that he was making it quite impossible for her to get away from him. He trapped her against a wall, with one arm each side of her. She felt so menaced that she thought for a moment she might faint.

'If you thought I was going to let you slap me, as you obviously wanted to, and make a public exhibition of both of us, you were wrong. You really have been making a play for Richard, have you? Or is that beneath your don't-touch idealism, too?' he asked roughly.

He didn't give her time to answer. One minute his shadowy face was glaring down at her. The next, his hands were firm on her shoulders and his mouth was hard on hers, bruising and forceful. It sent a fire coursing through her. She could feel the thudding of his heart, the long length of him pressed against her, the warm life of his lips drawing a response from her which should have been anger, but instead was a pulsing electrical force which made her weak at the knees and filled her with wild longing. She couldn't think, only feel, and her arms crept up around his neck as their bodies seemed to merge, the sense of his fingers tangling in her hair only right, his probing tongue bringing an answering sweetness from her parted lips. At that moment, she wanted it to go on forever . . .

A burst of laughter from somewhere inside the lighted hall woke both of them. And it was he who drew away first. He said, on a note which was, unbelievably, *laughter*, 'You shouldn't make me lose my temper. And you shouldn't be so kissable, either! Friends, my not-so-icy Cousin Kate?'

She pushed away from him. Memory had come back with a thump. Memory, and the urgent need to get away from him without showing anything. Without showing hurt at his lightness.

'No doubt you were only trying to prove a point, Cousin Nick,' she said. And if there was a tremor in her voice, he could take that for breathlessness. Or laughter like his own. 'Though what that point *was*, quite escapes me! Now, since I've had one hell of a day on duty, do you think you could let me go home? Because all I was thinking was that I had an excuse to go home now anyway.'

'I had a fairly late call myself. D'you want to be driven home? I've got my car here, and I expect you came with Tessa.'

Hearing him mention the other girl's name was an added sting. And a reminder. 'No, thanks, I've got my car here too,' Kate said, with a steadiness she could barely believe. 'Go back and—and enjoy the dance, why don't you?'

She walked past him, blind instinct telling her which way would lead her to the place where she'd parked her car a few short hours before. He didn't come after her. Why should he, after all? She didn't look round, though her hurried footsteps felt like flight and her hands were shaking when she found the car key in the small evening bag hanging on her wrist and fumbled it into the ignition. Was she going to spend all her life climbing into cars and driving away from Nick?

She felt as if she was driving far too jerkily as she came out of the university campus and began to thread her way through the broad streets. And her temper was coming back too, flaring hotly to cover hurt and shame and a deep, painful ache. How could he kiss her like that, and then laugh, and say, 'Friends?' How could he kiss her at all when he was involved with Tessa?

Because it hadn't meant anything to him, that was why. Because he was an untrustworthy, over-confident hulk, used to thinking *any* girl would be flattered by being in his arms. She had thought that about him the very first moment she saw him. Why, he probably thought she'd *liked* being kissed by him . . .

Kate found that she had almost missed the turning for Dendaa, swung the wheel abruptly, and hurtled into the side-turning at a speed which set her wheels bumping right on the edge of the drainage-ditch. She felt incredibly bad-tempered as she righted the car and made herself slow to a more decorous speed. There was no point in listening to that betraying whisper in her heart, telling her that things were quite hopeless anyway.

Quite aside from anything else, Tessa was in love with Nick and would probably manage to slip away from Richard's coffee-party in a little while to join him back at the dance. He was probably already romancing someone else by now, if he could find a woman who hadn't got a husband firmly in tow—since there were remarkably few single people among the Mutala expatriates. That was all he'd been doing with Kate—filling in an idle moment.

Misery wasn't exactly conducive to sleep, even after she'd managed to crawl into bed feeling drained and achey. Oh yes, just like flu! Why on earth couldn't she have felt like this about Richard? And why did it make her want to break into hysterical laughter to know that she never had? That it *had* just been 'adolescent hero worship' and brought her out all this way, too!

It was very late when she heard Tessa's car arrive and then her friend creeping in, humming. And Tessa only hummed when she was particularly happy.

Kate buried her head in the pillow to shut out the sound and to try to shut out her own utter loneliness, too.

CHAPTER SEVEN

IF KATE felt as if her life had been turned upside down, she took care not to show it. She spent the next two days, since they were days off, being busy and sociable; went to babysit for the Sinclairs so that they could go to the Holiday Inn and celebrate their wedding anniversary, on a long-standing promise, and offered to help the Barkers' nine-year-old son with his schoolwork because he was off school, recovering from a broken ankle. No one, seeing her brightness, would have imagined she had any problems at all. Somehow she and Tessa had managed not to discuss the dance at all, except to mention casually that it had made a change.

Kate was glad to go back on duty. She told herself that it was only becacuse she enjoyed her work, which she did—even the challenge of combating not only disease, but also ignorance and poverty. Most of the educated Lanbwena had their babies delivered privately and the pregnant white expatriates went down to Johannesburg to be delivered, so Mutala Hospital had more than its fair share of the poorer Africans.

Kate told herself that it wasn't that she wanted to be back in the hospital because she wanted to see Nick, wandering into the Unit while she did her night duty. She didn't want to see him at all, except to prove that she was going to treat him exactly the same as before. Whenever she and Tessa had been in the house at the same time, she had felt a jumpy expectation that the phone would ring and it would be him. He certainly hadn't rung while she was there, and Tessa didn't mention him either. Kate couldn't help being glad about that.

127

She went on duty to a busy night, during which Nick didn't appear. She hadn't needed to call in a doctor, but he hadn't come to do one of his rounds either. She told herself, bitterly, that he had obviously lost interest in obstetrics. And then reproved herself, knowing that he could well be busy. It didn't have to mean that he was having a night off, and seeing Tessa.

Then she passed him on her way off duty in the morning. Seeing him in the distance she hesitated for a moment, then made herself walk on so that she would pass the place where he stood discussing something with Dr Jeriku. As she came up to them she said, 'Good morning,' casually, with a smile which included both men, and in a voice which sounded bright enough to show that she didn't have anything against anybody.

She was aware of Nick swinging round, of his voice saying, 'Oh, hallo,' on a note which might have sounded a little warmer than his usual tones, if she let herself think about it. But she was too glad to be past, looking brisk, to dwell on it, and she heard Dr Jeriku going on with whatever he had been saying, so Nick obviously wasn't coming after her . . .

The next night she had a call-out which, although it wasn't a distant one, kept her out of the Unit during the hours when a doctor might do a casual round. On the next, Nick looked in on the ward while she was doing a delivery and, naturally enough, had gone again before she had finished.

Then on the fourth night he didn't come into the ward again, probably because he had been in it just before she came off duty, as Kate had noted bitterly from the records. Oh, blast the man! How could she show him that she meant to treat him casually if she didn't see him? And she was starting her nights-off tomorrow . . .

He was, however, standing on the edge of the car park when she came off shift in the morning. Standing apparently doing nothing except staring into space.

Kate felt an immediate and contrary urge to invent an errand which would take her away until he had finished waiting for whoever he was waiting for. She made herself walk on instead, trying to suppress a deep yearning which hit her just at the sight of him. She ought to have been feeling angry and feeding her resentment with all the unkind thoughts she had ever had about him, reminding herself that that casual lounging figure was someone she could never trust, but somehow all of that simply seemed to settle down into a dull ache. However, she certainly wasn't going to show it. As she came up to him he smiled at her, and she smiled back and said brightly,

'No early clinic for once? No wards screaming for you, either?'

'Neither at the moment, so I took the chance to come and wait for you. We don't seem to have seen each other all this week. I'm off duty tonight, though, and you'll have nights off. How about coming out with me for a drink?'

'Oh, sorry, I've got an appointment to go out to supper and listen to some records.' It was almost true, though it had actually been a casual suggestion from Elizabeth Rouse to go round and join in a family meal if she felt like it. 'In fact I'm tied up all through my nights off,' she found herself saying with a gaiety which, even to her, sounded a little too brittle. She saw his eyebrows go up, and added quickly, 'That's the way it is!'

'You've gone uptight again. Do you put it on with the uniform?' he asked teasingly, and with far too charming a smile. 'Now, why would that be?'

'Tiredness,' Kate said promptly. 'I'm thoroughly glad to get off duty and I'm dying to get some sleep, actually, so—'

'I won't keep you, then. You sound almost high. Lack of sleep?' He was giving her far too considering a look. 'I suppose your date tonight wouldn't be at the university?'

'Goodness no, why should it be?' The urge to see Richard's name as a defence came, but as quickly died. Nick was a colleague of Richard's, after all. And, besides, she wasn't going to risk him going back to his taunts, as the sudden mockery in his eyes suggested he might—taunts which had too much past truth in them, as she was bitterly aware. Kate went on rapidly, knowing she had flushed but trying for a laugh, 'I don't know where you get your over-imaginative ideas from.'

'Or why I have to show so much curiosity about your affairs?' he asked. And then he stretched and added coolly, 'We'll have a drink another time, when you're not so busy. Pity about tonight. Go on and get your sleep, then!'

He was turning away so that, luckily, he couldn't have seen the wistfulness which might have shown in her eyes—the sudden desire to change her mind and say that she *would* go out with him after all. Kate pulled herself together rapidly and told herself crossly that she wasn't supposed to be feeling like that. Tessa was her best friend.

It didn't help, then, to wake up in the evening and find a note from Tessa to say that she'd gone out to supper. Kate knew she must have gone out with Nick.

It was easy enough to find plenty to do with her nights off, anyway, so that she was rarely in the house. Then she went back on duty to bury herself in work and to treat Nick purely as a doctor who came to the ward.

Luckily she managed to become quite adroit at not running into him around the hospital site, if only by keeping herself briskly in motion and never taking a short cut past the doctors' houses and never going into the canteen. And leaving her car parked in different places, too, just in case . . .

She thought Nick gave her a puzzled look once or

twice when they did have to meet, but after a couple of days she was aware that he had started taking the same impersonal tone in speaking to her as she did to him. Then it was time off again, and then night duty. And when he did come in for a round she was always busy. When he came in because she'd called for a doctor, she was heartily glad to see him, of course, and, betrayingly, glad of the excuse to be with him. If only for the chance to stand and watch his face as he frowned thoughtfully over a patient or see him smile at her with shared relief over some problem which they managed to solve together.

Tessa was looking happier, Kate reminded herself rigidly. At least that meant that everything was turning out well for somebody. From the look of her and her tendency to hum, maybe she'd even announce her engagement to Nick soon. Or something. Kate didn't hesitate when Nick paused casually in the Unit doorway one day and suggested, again, that she had a drink with him sometime when they were free. Even if the invitation had almost sounded brotherly, she invented a quick excuse which was firm enough to be a definite no. She was disconcerted when he said,

'All right, I'll leave this here for you, then. Don't open it till you go off duty, though.'

The envelope he handed her was medium-sized and stiffened. Kate stared at it, wondering numbly what it could be. Then she had to put it down on the desk to go and see to a patient. It was quite a lot later before she had the chance to glance at the package lying there on the desk with her name written on the outside in Nick's neat but firm handwriting. It made her feel a little wary. And why mustn't she open it until she went off duty?

She had a quiet moment now, so she slit the envelope open carefully. Inside, there was a carefully-enlarged photograph. She felt quickly in the envelope to see if

he had put a challenging message in with it, but he
hadn't. He had simply written *David Raven* neatly on
the back, with a date. Was it a challenge? Or just a
piece of kindness?

Kate swallowed and slipped the photograph back into
its envelope quickly as a trainee came into view. He'd
probably thought she'd burst into tears all over the Unit,
but of course she wouldn't. And she would keep the
photograph, too, gratefully—though she was hit by the
wildly ironic knowledge that she had thought the envelope might contain . . . What? An invitation to his and
Tessa's engagement party? Surely not! Even Tessa
couldn't be too shy to tell her herself! And it was painful
not to know whether Nick's gesture was to take a dig
at her, or whether it was done out of the same kindness
he showed to the patients.

It was to take a dig at her, obviously. That became
plain the following night when he eyed her across the
prem he had just finished examining and asked abruptly,
'Well, did you tear it up?'

'What? Oh, no. I was glad to have it. And thank you
for getting it done for me,' Kate said carefully. And
then, 'Will you sign this chart, please, to say this one
can go on to straight three-hourly feeds instead of glu-
cose and water?'

'Yes, here.' He scribbled his signature on the clip-
board she was holding out to him and then paused long
enough to make her look up at him. 'Friends, then?' he
asked.

'Yes, of course!'

'Then why, I wonder, has it been so difficult to get
anywhere near you?' he asked, smiling at her.

'Goodness, it hasn't, has it? After all, I've been here,
rushing around the ward in a non-stop fashion. Well,
except for the day I did the ante-natal clinic with Mr
Olinga,' Kate said precisely. 'Has Tessa been complain-
ing that I'm hardly ever in when I'm off duty? Well, it

does get like that—there seem to be so many things to do!' And with that she had the chance to escape, because a trainee came up the ward with a message that Casualty was ringing round for a doctor and wanted Dr Kyle particularly because it was a patient he had seen before.

And just as well too, with Nick standing there smiling at her like that and sounding as if he had actually been trying to get-hold of her. The idea drove Kate out of the Dendaa house even more thoroughly than ever, particularly on her nights off.

One day she realised that the dance had been a month ago and that she had neither seen nor thought of Richard since then, except to ask after him from Tessa, and then only because she was trying to sound as she supposed she had always sounded. It was ironic that he could vanish so completely out of her thoughts when she looked back at the Kate who had arrived here. Ironic, too, to hear Sally say sympathetically that it must be rather boring for her with so few bachelors around, and that they must try to find someone for her. Kate made a light, laughing answer and then found herself thinking bitterly that it really was a pity there weren't a few more bachelors around Mutala—or dozens of them, even. If there were, she might, surely, find a cure for feeling drawn to one, in particular!

She'd been in Lanbwe three months, she found in surprise when she counted it up, knowing that it felt more like for ever. She hardly seemed to recognise the Kate who had come out here, precise and reserved and used to working by the book, when she looked back at herself.

Now, with an increasing if rudimentary vocabulary of Lanbwena words of her own, she could talk to some of her patients without the need of much interpretation—unless they talked quickly or tried to say anything too complicated. She was used to call-outs and delivering babies where there were no facilities at all. She was used to a wide empty blue sky and flat country and thorn trees. And constant sunshine. She was used to wrapping up warmly at night, too, even if it was difficult to believe that this was now Lanbwe's mid-winter, when the day-time temperatures were still pleasantly warm and families were still going off for weekend picnics at the Dam.

It was certainly a cold night when she was called out of the theatre where she was waiting as duty midwife while Nick did a Caesarean. Watching him operate was a pleasure Kate wasn't prepared to deny herself and she had, anyway, been glad that he was there to do it. She pushed away the memory that Tessa had gone back to saying, 'Nick says . . .' all the time.

Tessa had been packing to set off on ten days' field-work, going off into the bush areas with Richard because he apparently needed to gather some more statistics. She seemed quite cheerful about going off into the wilds to sleep under canvas. But of course, she had done it before . . .

There was certainly no need for Kate to be thinking about all this while she waited to see what had obstructed the baby which Nick would shortly release from the mother's distended abdomen. It hadn't been possible to decide just what the trouble was, but normal labour had been going on far too long for things to be left alone.

Part of Kate's mind flickered to the Unit because it was still her responsibility while she was in Theatre. When Isaac's face appeared at the door she looked round sharply, then moved quietly to see what crisis might have come up in her absence.

'Urgent message from Old Katedi,' he muttered to her, looking more alarmed than necessary, and with his eyes sliding beyond her to see how the Caesarean was going. 'No time to come into hospital, labour far advanced.'

'All right, I'll come.' Kate stepped outside the Theatre and slipped off her mask. 'You gown up and come in here instead of me. You've done quite a lot of theatre work, haven't you? This baby may need resuscitating, but don't get worried about it, you've got Dr Kyle.' She made her voice deliberately bracing to give Isaac confidence.

The husband, who had arrived by bicycle, was worried and said his wife had been in labour for hours. Kate forbore to ask him why they hadn't brought her into hospital earlier, rang through for an ambulance and appointed the most efficient of the trainees to run things in her absence, reminding her to write everything down so that Kate could countersign it on her return. Petal, she decided, would be the trainee she took with her. She was a nice-natured girl who never panicked about anything. The two of them picked up the equipment and Kate decided that she hadn't time to change out of her theatre-tunic so she would have to go as she was. It wasn't far, anyway.

She was rather sorry she hadn't at least gathered up her cloak, not to mention thick socks and a blanket to wrap round herself, as they hurried out to the ambulance and the sharp chill in the air caught her. It had been warm in theatre and she'd forgotten what it would be like to be outside for long in nothing but thin clothes. However, the woman's husband was already flinging his bicycle up on to the ambulance's roof-rack, which seemed to be there for just that purpose, and Kate could hardly say that she wanted to hold things up just because she was cold. The inside of the ambulance cut off the wind, anyway, and she had to make a calm assessment of what they might find ahead of them.

If the labour had been going on for hours, and the pains had reached the point of being almost continuous, they'd probably have to deliver on the spot, unless there were complications. Old Katedi was Mutala's only slum, with its mixture of traditional mud-huts and shacks crowded close together along streets of beaten earth. There was no running water there, either, except standpipes set here and there. Still, at least it wasn't a first baby.

The ambulance gave a sudden jolt and the engine coughed and died. Petal, sitting placidly wrapped in her cloak over a cardigan on top of her white uniform, began to move, but Kate could hear the ambulance driver pulling on the starter, so they obviously hadn't arrived yet. The engine whined, coughed, and died again. There was a rattle and a thump as the driver got out, and then the scrape of the bonnet being lifted. Kate heard an anxious chatter from the husband, and a moment or two later the driver pulled the rear door of the ambulance open.

'Sorry, Nurses, we've broken down. I think the petrol feed-pipe's broken. There doesn't seem to be much I can do.'

'How near are we?' Kate peered out past him. The dim light showed her they were into the edge of Old Katedi. 'All right,' she said rapidly, 'it can't be far, so Nurse and I will walk the rest of the way. Can you find a phone and ring the hospital?'

'Can't leave the ambulance. Not round here. They'd even have the wheels off.'

'Oh, yes, of course. Well, we'll have to go on ahead anyway.' She could see that the husband, who had come round to join the driver at the door, was in a renewed state of panic. 'Tell him we'll walk to his house and see about the ambulance later,' she instructed Petal, because it was easier than trying out her own halting words of Lanbwena. She then left the girl to it as she checked that they had got the delivery pack, bag, and transfusion equipment. Between them, they could carry whatever might be needed. The only trouble would lie in getting the mother, or mother and baby, back to the hospital.

It was no real distance to walk. The husband led the way at a fast lope through the roadways lit only here and there by the gleam of a lamp from a hump-shaped hut. Stars sprinkled the sky high above to give at least a dim radiance, though there was no moon. They took several twists and turns which were probably short-cuts, through places which would have been too narrow for the ambulance. Sometimes, Kate felt sure, cutting across someone's rudimentary garden-plot, as she stubbed her toe against a piece of low fencing and nearly fell over a sleeping hen.

She wished she was in something thicker than her theatre clothes, and had begun to shiver with the cold. She could only see Petal by the girl's white cap showing up sharply on top of her dark head, but the trainee was moving along placidly, exchanging the occasional word with the husband, which was probably to tell him not to get too far ahead, from the tone of her voice. They came out on to a wider piece of road again and stopped abruptly in front of a shack, one of the square ones, apparently quite stoutly-built under a corrugated-iron roof, and with the light of something which looked bright enough to be a hurricane lamp gleaming from its square, curtained window.

'Here, Staff Nurse,' Petal said, and stood aside for Kate to go in first.

She opened the wooden door wondering what she would find, but the scene inside was remarkably tranquil. Two very small children lay asleep together in a truckle-bed against one wall, under thin but apparently clean blankets. Other sparse furniture looked perhaps a little lop-sided on the earth floor, but an attempt had been made to brighten the place up with pieces of material tacked up to divide the space, and the hurricane lamp was giving warmth as well as light. As she stepped inside, an African woman in a cotton frock and cardigan, her head covered in a scarf, turned round swiftly with a finger to her lips, and then a half-toothed smile when she saw who it was. Since she wasn't at all pregnant she must be the grandmother, and her look of pleased satisfaction seemed to be justified as she drew a curtain aside, beginning a soft explanation in Lanbwena too fast for Kate to follow.

'She says the baby was born half an hour ago.' Kate could see that without Petal's translation, because the young mother was fast asleep on a low bed with the infant, carefully-wrapped, tucked into the curve of her arm. She let Petal go on translating the details. Everything was satisfactory, apparently, and the grandmother had delivered the baby herself.

Kate stepped to the bedside, smiled round at the grandmother, and then knelt down to make a swift examination of the infant. She seemed to be an entirely healthy little girl, probably about seven pounds in weight, and the cord had been properly tied off. Kate checked it, gave it a quick dusting of sterile powder to be going on with, and wrapped the baby up again. The placenta had come away satisfactorily too, apparently, and the grandmother had kept it to show them, so that Kate could feel, with relief, that their arrival had scarcely been necessary at all.

'Please tell her she's done splendidly, and I can see she's delivered lots of babies before. It looks as if all we've got to do is examine the mother, take down all the details, and give her a syntometrine injection.' That was routine, to cut down any danger of late bleeding. And then, of course, since there didn't seem to be any crisis here, they'd got to face the problem of getting mother and child back to the hospital for the forty-eight hour admission which Sister insisted on, no matter whether her midwives had actually delivered the baby or not.

First, though, they must wake the young mother up gently so that she could be examined, and make a note of all the details she and the grandmother could give them. That took time, though everything seemed to be as satisfactory as the birth had been.

The other children stirred a little and were hushed gently back to sleep by their grandmother. The father came into the shack at last and seemed pleased to have a new daughter. He had been hanging about outside and Kate had almost forgotten about him, so used was she now to the habit of banning men from a hut during a birth. It had made her wonder occasionally how the older Lanbwena women viewed the male trainee mid-wives, but they seemed to take it for granted that they must be doctors. The routines over, she sat back on her heels and looked up at Petal.

'If the driver can't leave the ambulance, we'll have to go and find a phone, I suppose, and ring in for another ambulance to take us all back. I think, though, we'll go and see if he has managed to mend things after all. Could you explain why we're leaving, and say that we will be back to pick mother and baby up? Oh, and,' she gave a wry grin, 'ask the father to guide us back, would you? I don't think I'd ever find the way!'

It seemed shorter going back, but Kate was sharply aware of the cold again. She tried to hide her shivers and had to restrain impatience when the driver, still with his immobilised ambulance, expressed doubt that there was a phone in Old Katedi at all. Eventually it seemed to be decided that there was one in the slaughterhouse, but it would mean waking the night-watchman up to get to it. Then there was a further long discussion, culminating in the decision that the father wouldn't be official enough, and the driver couldn't by the rules leave his ambulance in charge of anybody, so Kate and Petal would have to go to the slaughterhouse themselves. The father directed them there because it was only round two corners, but then disappeared, either to go back to his wife, or to wait with the driver— Kate wasn't sure which.

The slaughterhouse was a large concrete building with high half-walls, a corrugated-iron roof, and a lot of protective wire and padlocks to stop anyone breaking in. It took a good ten minutes of banging and shouting to bring the night-watchman out. He emerged so sleepily that Kate could see how he viewed his job! There were another ten minutes of forceful argument before he would unlock everything and let them in.

Kate glanced enviously in through the open doorway of the tiny room in which he spent his nights. She could even see an electric bar fire glowing in there, let alone a camp-bed and a pile of blankets. She felt crossly that he might have invited them in there, when she must be looking blue with cold. He didn't, however. Having shown them the phone fixed to one wall, he said grumpily that they could wait inside the warehouse building if they must, and then withdrew into his warm shelter and shut the door behind him.

The phone was working and Kate got through to the Maternity Unit without difficulty. She found herself talking to Isaac, and explained the problem to him. Could he send another ambulance out as quickly as possible? Then, unexpectedly, she heard Nick's familiar voice come on the line.

'Crisis?' he asked.

'No, the delivery was fine, already done before we got here. But the ambulance had broken down so we can't get back.' Kate found herself letting out a shaky laugh. 'It's not that it's urgent from the patient's point of view, it's me. I haven't got enough on, and I'm frozen. I went straight out from theatre.'

'Silly girl. We'd better get you rescued as soon as possible, hadn't we? Give me the phone number where you are now, in case of any problems.' She gave it to him, and he went on, 'Got anything to wrap yourself in?'

'No. I expect I'll live.' Somehow the sound of his voice was warming her, just a little, already. 'Nick,' she said swiftly, using his name quite unthinkingly, 'are there problems there? Why are you in the Unit? Have all sorts of things come up while I'm out?'

'No, it's all quiet, don't worry. I just hung around to keep an eye on things.'

'What happened with the Caesar?'

'All OK. I've told you, nothing to worry about! We'll get you picked up from the slaughterhouse as quickly as we can. A *slaughterhouse*?' he said on a chuckle, and then the line clicked off and he was gone.

There was nothing to do then but wait, and if Kate caught herself in a ridiculous glow of pleasure just because she had heard that deep, friendly voice, she could tell herself that at least it warmed her up a little. Petal suddenly woke up to the fact that her staff nurse was cold and offered a share of her cloak. The two girls huddled together in the draughty building, staying near the phone in case the hospital rang back with different instructions.

Now and again the night-watchman popped his head out to see if they were still there and looked very much as if he would like to have turned off the one electric bulb which cast a bleak light around the large, empty, concrete-floored area he was supposed to supervise. Petal, sounding extremely human and not nearly as proper as the Lanbwena girls usually were, murmured an impolite description of him which set both of them off into suppressed giggles.

A banging on the door came at last, and when the night-watchman shuffled out to unlock everything all over again, Kate was confused to see that it wasn't just the new ambulance driver outside. Nick was there too, standing beside his car. He came towards her with a grin, and before she knew what he was going to do, he had stripped off his thick sweater and was pulling it over her head.

'Get into this.' He was helping her to get her arms into the sleeves as she emerged, and giving her a quick rub, too, to warm her up. 'No, *I* won't be cold, if that's what you're trying to say, because I haven't just spent several hours being chilled, have I?'

'You don't know how grateful I am for that!' His body-warmth was still in the wool, too, so that it was like being wrapped in immediate comfort. 'We'd better find our way back to the patient again, not that she actually needed us at all.'

'I suggest you send your trainee to pick her up, then. You and I could go and check on the broken-down ambulance.'

'I can find the way all right,' Petal said surprisingly, beford Kate could ask. 'I know where it is. We left all the equipment in the other ambulance, Staff Nurse, so if I go and get the patient, you could collect that. It would save time.'

'Oh, yes. Go straight back with her, then, will you? And do a proper admission when you get her there.' Kate smiled at the girl, who had remained her pleasant self throughout all the mixed events of the call-out, and decided that she could certainly trust her to see the mother and new baby back to the hospital safely. A moment later Petal was gone, and Kate was getting into Nick's car so that he could turn it and go in search of the hospital's broken-down vehicle.

Nick took a quick look at the ambulance and told the driver he'd better sleep in it for the rest of the night and someone would come out and do running repairs in the morning. It was three-thirty already, Kate discovered with a surprised look at her watch, and it had been well before midnight when they were called out. Nick, she thought suddenly, wouldn't get any sleep at all.

Her mind flicked over sharply to wonder what had been going on in the Unit in her absence. They were back in the car by then, the precious equipment retrieved, and Kate turned to ask him a swift question.

'Has everything really been all right in Maternity while I was gone?'

'Sure. Why, do you think I couldn't cope?'

The teasing note in his voice made her giggle. 'All right, I know,' she answered him back. 'You're going to say you've delivered more babies than I've had hot dinners.'

'A fair few. No, actually, your trainees have been coping perfectly well. There weren't any crises, and you can stop worrying. I didn't just say it so that you wouldn't fret.'

'Oh, I stopped fretting the minute I knew you were there.' She said the words lightly, but found herself glancing at him with a sudden feeling of shyness. 'It—it was very nice of you to come out.'

'Oh, I couldn't leave you unrescued, could I? Freezing to death in a slaughterhouse . . .'

'You wouldn't find that so funny if you'd had to wake up an evil-tempered night-watchman to get in there in the first place,' Kate retorted, though with an echo of his amusement in her voice. 'And why do you find it so funny, anyway?' she added in mock-indignation.

'I don't know, it just is. Maybe it's the right place to find lethal ladies?' He glanced at her, and suddenly she felt a tingling sensation coming to disturb the relaxation she had been feeling with him. 'No answer to that?' he enquired silkily.

'I was trying to frame something pompous like, "I bring life *into* the world so you can't call me lethal"—' She tried to make her words sound light-hearted rather than uncertain. And then she saw that they were already turning into the hospital site, and was half glad, half sorry. Glad because she ought to be, sorry because there was a tempting excitement in the racing of her pulse. 'Since we're here, you'd better have your sweater back,' she said quickly. 'Thank you very much for the loan.'

'No, keep it on, you'll only get cold again if you take it off and I've got another.' He drew up in a space near Maternity, empty of the usual stretchers and wheelchairs which were left there in the day-time, and turned to face her. 'Are you warmer? Because, if not—'

'I'm gradually thawing. You'd better go and get some sleep, hadn't you?'

'I can think of things I want more,' he said, and his hands came out to pull her against him, while his lips found hers unerringly in a kiss of such passionate sweetness that she was drowning in it.

Her body seemed to catch fire as his hands moved over her to draw all the response she had been holding back, and she clung to him with a wild, yearning longing which brought a thunder to her ears and a melting sensation to her bones . . .

'Kate,' he murmured against her hair. His lips found hers again, burning into her for a moment which was too brief, because it gave her the chance to remember too many things as he spoke again, huskily. 'Listen, you darling, beautiful girl—'

'Let me alone.' The words came out raw and bald and breathless and it was like tearing off a limb to make herself be angry with him, when his voice had been urgent with the longing she herself felt. 'You've had your thanks,' she said, whipping herself up into anger as a defence. She pulled away to scrabble in the back seat, reaching for the equipment because it was the best way she knew to hide the fact that her eyes were stinging with tears. Tessa; she *had* to remember Tessa.

'My what?'

'You heard me! No, let me go—I'm trying to reach

the delivery pack, which goodness knows I may need a lot more than I need *this*!'

'Oh, go ahead then, scream and run.' There was such exasperation in his voice, and such disgust, that it hurt unbearably. He had pulled the car door open in a quick movement, and was out of it. A second later he had yanked Kate's door open and was practically pulling her out, reaching into the car to pile her with the things she had been trying to reach.

'Thanks,' she said stiffly, and tried not to flinch at his expression, all too visible in the lights which lit the walkways between the wards. She wanted to say something else, but she couldn't think of anything, so she turned on her heel and stalked away from him.

She could have yelled at him that he was an opportunist. She could have said all sorts of things, if she hadn't felt so numb with loss that she didn't even know where she was putting her feet. She could, a guilty whisper inside her head suggested, simply have forgotten all about everything including Tessa—because hadn't somebody said, *All's fair in love or war*?

CHAPTER EIGHT

SHE COULDN'T go on convincing herself that there was any doubt about the way she was feeling about Nick. Somewhere along the line she seemed to have fallen for him hook, line and sinker.

She would have to hide it. She would have to try to conceal, too, the fact that their last confrontation had left her feeling so bruised. She would have to resist the temptation to reach for the phone and call him. He'd probably only say something nasty, anyway, considering the way they'd parted.

She certainly seemed to have put him off satisfactorily, because he was cold and remote and very much the boss when she was forced to run into him in the hospital. It reminded her of the early days. He seemed to come into Maternity as little as possible when Kate was there, and when he did have to come in she was aware that he avoided looking directly at her. That hurt, when she ought to have been glad about it. And it hurt even more to see him turn and go in another direction if he caught sight of her on the walkways.

Kate had returned his sweater by wrapping it up and labelling it and leaving it in the staff canteen. She had felt a ridiculous longing to keep it because it was his. She'd spent a long time wondering idiotically why she'd ever thought fair-haired, grey-eyed men weren't her type at all, and she kept catching herself out in guilty daydreams in which they hadn't quarrelled, or had made it up, and there wasn't anything at all to prevent their going on from there . . .

She found she was snappy with the trainees on the ward, and less patient than she ought to have been with the mothers, too. It was almost a relief when two days of electrical storms gave her an excuse for being jumpy. There was no rain, but an endless crackling in the air and heavy crashes of thunder to follow vivid bursts of lightning. It was enough to unnerve anybody, and sent several of the mothers into labour early too, so that there was a sudden rush of births and call-outs, as well as extra work in the Prem Unit because the hospital electricity kept on blinking off and a special eye had to be kept on the incubator babies.

The storms were caused by, 'Something bumping into something over the Kalahari Desert,' according to Dr Achmed, who had come into the ward while Kate was coping with the premature delivery of a mother who was running a fever and who was looking, too, as if she might haemorrhage. Kate found herself longing for Nick's reliable, reassuring presence as she fought to stimulate the tiny baby into breathing on its own while keeping a wary eye on the mother. And if she longed for Nick a great deal too often, at least this time she had a good reason for it.

She obviously needed a cure for being in love with the wrong man, she decided bitterly when the storms rumbled away into the distance, the weather brightened again, and everybody else felt better except her. She needed distraction.

She needed it still more on the day when she came off duty to find that Tessa was back. It was a different Tessa, bright-eyed and sparkling and looking not just pretty but almost beautiful—lit up with a tremulous excitement which seemed to make her keep breaking out in a Cheshire-cat grin.

'Hallo, Katie,' she said, obviously trying to sound casual, but failing totally. 'I'm afraid I'm not back for long, only an hour or two in fact, because we're going off to Jo'burg for about three weeks, and probably getting married while we're there!' she blurted out in a sudden breathless rush.

'You're what?'

'Richard's asked me to marry him. Oh, Katie!' Tessa was bright pink. 'I thought he only saw me as part of the furniture. I thought . . . Well, I'm sure he was carrying on with Gina Harvey, for all he says it was just that she was making a dead set at him, but, oh Katie, he says it was me all along! That he's not too vague to have noticed me, but he just couldn't afford to muck up a good working relationship!' She gave a giggle suddenly, and did a little twirl as if she couldn't possibly keep still.

'That's what coming to Africa does for you,' she said, on another laugh, adding, 'I wasn't in love with him before we came out here. I just thought he was nice but exasperating.'

'*Tess*,' Kate said faintly, trying to stem this extraordinary tide of words. It was difficult to take any of it in. 'I thought,' she said on a stammer, 'I thought you were in love with Nick?'

'Did you?' Tessa said, stopping to stare at her, round-eyed. 'Why? It's funny you should say that, though,' she said with another giggle, 'because it was seeing me with Nick at the dance which—which sort of brought Richard to the point. First he thought Nick was giving me a present when he saw him giving me back my bracelet, and he'd only been mending the catch for me! And then, Richard says, he had to sit and watch while I was dancing with him. Not that he said anything then, he just sort of started looking possessive. Katie, you don't have to stare at me in quite that surprised way, do you?'

'Sorry,' Kate said rapidly, because Tessa had stopped to gaze at her with an almost guilty look. 'I—I mean, congratulations! I'm absolutely delighted for you, it's just that,' she gulped, and went on with difficulty, 'you didn't say anything.'

'Well, I thought he was getting interested in *you*.' Tessa gave her a shamefaced look. 'Yet another blonde catching his attention, you know? I'm sorry, I must have seemed absolutely horrid, but it *felt* horrid, being jealous of you, of all people. Oh God, I must tell Nick that it wasn't like that at all, but I just haven't seen him lately!'

She didn't seem to notice the way Kate stiffened, because she was going on. 'I must tell him if I can get hold of him before I go! I can't wait to see his face. I'm not going to write him a note though, I want to *see* him when I tell him that it's all come out right after all!'

'He—he knows all about it, does he?'

'Yes.' Tessa looked awkward again, as far as it was possible for her to do so, with happiness surfacing through every pore. 'I cried on his shoulder once. It was only just after we'd met, too. It just happened. But he was sweet about it. He even said . . . I shouldn't really tell you this, but I will, just to show you how nice he can be. He said he knew what it was like to be stuck with an impossible love which just wouldn't go away, because the girl *he* went around with for years and years went off and married his best friend instead, and he still couldn't manage to forget her. He said, to cheer me up, that at least it had the advantage of making him fireproof. He even offered to try to distract Gina Harvey, if it would help!' She gave a gurgle of laughter. 'I should imagine anyone might fall for Nick, if he really chose to turn on the charm.'

'Did it work in this case?' Kate asked through stiff lips.

'Well, no, actually, because I told him not to. But he said the offer was always open. There you are, you see. I told you he was really nice. But I'm supposed to be packing! Katie, do come and talk to me while I do it, and tell me what to take.'

'I would, but I'm babysitting for the Rouses,' Kate said, suddenly remembering. She was stunned, so it was just as well Tessa was in no state to recognise it. Tessa and *Richard*? It made sense as soon as it was pointed out. But it wasn't that which was ringing in her mind like a cold knell. It was all the other things Tessa had said.

'Look, I'm really sorry to have to go,' she told Tessa, somehow managing to put warmth and pleasure at her friend's happiness into her voice. That, at least, was real. 'I'm so glad for you, honestly. I'm sure you really suit each other. Will you give him my congratulations? And, oh, Tess, do be happy—not that I need to say that, from the look of you!'

Tessa gave her a sparkling grin by way of answer, accepted the hug Kate gave her, and danced off into her room to pack. And Kate went away into her own room to change rapidly, trying to keep her mind empty until she could get out of the house.

Richard Cranshaw seemed to have led a much more adventurous life than Kate would ever have imagined of him. But it wasn't that which was echoing round and round in her head.

Anyone might fall for Nick if he chose to turn on the charm. And offering to 'distract' Gina Harvey, or anyone who might look as if they were threatening to offer competition to Tessa. Offering himself casually from the lordly position of being 'fireproof'. Even, and apparently unbeknown to Tessa, going through with it *this* time . . .

It was just as well the Rouses' two young children were good sleepers, because Kate didn't know how she would have coped calmly with them against the fury which rose and rose in her. It was easy enough to hate Nicholas Kyle just now, easy to remember every evil thought she'd ever had about him. Conceited, arrogant, untrustworthy, consciously charming. And he'd put on that charm deliberately, offered friendship . . . And she had fallen for it!

Well, at least he couldn't know that. She could gather the rags of her pride about her—though she didn't know how she was going to face him the next time they met, knowing what she knew now.

It didn't help Kate to get back from a long evening to find Tessa gone and a note propped up on the table. The note, hastily scribbled, said, *Couldn't get hold of Nick, but don't tell him the news when you see him, please? I want to tell him myself, and we're keeping the news secret until we get back. Bless you, love, Tess.*

It did at least help Kate a little to know that her two days off were just starting, so that she had time to drag herself together before she had to go into the hospital again. Even if she knew she would spend that time brooding and bitterly going over Tessa's words, and even more bitterly remembering Nick's give-away attitude at the dance, at least she didn't have to see him. When she looked back further she could see the calculation in his every move, ever since the day she had run into him at the university. A bitter anger fanned the cold, betrayed feeling of desolation inside her, but at least she had her pride and could tell herself that it was laughable to imagine that she had ever thought she was in love with Nick. She'd just been bored, stirred up by being in Africa—oh, all sorts of things . . .

When Sally Barker rang up to say that she knew it was short notice, but could Kate come to dinner this evening to meet a barrister friend of James's who had arrived out here on an unexpected visit, Kate was all too ready to accept. Sally dropped it in, carefully, that James's friend was unmarried and had come out to give legal advice to the Lanbwena government on the drafting of changes in the Constitution. Kate didn't care what he did, it was a distraction, wasn't it? And if the word had bitter overtones, she was prepared to crush them and dress up in a pretty but casual cotton frock, and go round to the Barkers' house glitteringly ready to be as sociable as possible.

She told herself that this was what she had been missing—available male company. And it was amazing how stupid one could get, where there was a shortage of it.

James's friend seemed a pleasant enough man. He seemed to like the look of Kate, too, eyeing her with appreciation when they were introduced. He was called Philip Hickley and he had dark curly hair and hazel eyes and a very smooth manner. If he had a rather annoying laugh, and a tendency to tell long legal stories which always seemed to prove how much cleverer he was than anyone else, Kate decided that one couldn't have everything. When he ended the evening by suggesting that the two of them should make a date to have dinner together at the Holiday Inn the following night, Kate agreed with smiling promptness.

He came to pick her up in the Barkers' car. Kate had spent a lot of time and thought in deciding what to wear. She'd finally chosen a close-fitting, satiny-looking blue sheath dress with a short-sleeved matching jacket, which she'd bought in a Mutala boutique but not worn so far. It seemed like a good idea to dress up for Philip Hickley since she had gained the impression that he liked to be smart. She'd thought about piling her hair up on top of her head, then remembered that he was only a couple of inches taller than she was and left it loose instead. The look of admiring approval he gave her when she arrived proved that she'd been right in dressing up rather than wearing something more casual, and he himself was wearing a dark suit. He looked round the house with interest as she let him in.

'All these houses are much the same, aren't they? It's surprising how different they look, though, with different people's possessions in them. Do you have this one to yourself?'

'No, I share it, but my friend Tessa's away at the moment. The African mask and statue are hers—she's travelled around quite a bit.'

'I suppose there's plenty of room for two girls, without getting too much on top of each other,' he said with a smile. 'Rather more than there is for a family.'

'The Barkers have one more bedroom than we do. Would you like a sherry before we go?'

'Thank you, but whisky's my tipple. You don't keep it? Never mind, let's make our way and do our drinking there.'

Kate hadn't been to the Holiday Inn except to swim and for the occasional drink in the bar afterwards. Going there for the evening showed her a different crowd, and the wide bar was busy with people—mainly, it seemed, groups of men, though there were couples too, and one large mixed party which seemed to be celebrating something. There was a lot of noise, and the floor-length windows which were usually left open during the day had been shut for night-time and swathed off with heavy, plush-looking curtains.

Philip seemed to be the sort of person who had no difficulty in catching a barman's eye and he provided Kate unasked with a champagne cocktail, telling her with smooth gallantry that it was the only thing a girl with her looks should be drinking. He then sank three whiskies himself while Kate was still sipping from her one glass, and she decided he must have a hard head.

He wasn't difficult to talk to, anyway, because he did most of the talking himself. All she really had to do was listen attentively and smile now and again. His smooth manner made him seem quite good-looking, she decided firmly, and she really shouldn't be noticing that he had rather a long upper lip and that his mouth seemed to be too full of teeth. She wished she could feel as animated as the people all round them, and tried to feel bright and interested and full of enjoyment.

'There seems to be a shortage of women in Mutala,' Philip commented, looking round the room. His gaze came back to Kate, smiling at her contemplatively. 'I don't imagine you mind being in the minority though, do you?'

'The people here aren't Mutala residents. I think a lot of people must stay here on business, coming in for short trips.'

'Like myself,' he said agreeably. 'James and Sally told me people also come and stay here for the gambling. They've quite a large casino, haven't they? Do you play?'

'I never have. It just hasn't particularly come my way.'

'Oh well, I must introduce you to it, then. You can't go very far wrong with roulette. No doubt the casino adds its piece to the country's economy,' he added, looking round again and fingering his empty glass absently. 'They don't seem to be very speedy about finding us our table in the dining-room. Is the food here as good as I'm assured it is?'

'I suppose it depends what else you've got to compare it with,' Kate said airily, suddenly unwilling to admit that she didn't dine out here all the time. She was supposed to be fascinating this man, after all. 'It's really the only place,' she went on, 'though of course it is part of an international chain, which helps!'

'Rather different for you after London. Still, I should imagine you're in great demand. There, as well as here!'

'I'm a working girl, though. Nursing takes up a lot of one's time and energy,' Kate told him, wishing he wouldn't smile so much and show all those teeth.

'But not all of it, I'm sure! Now what, I wonder,

makes a very beautiful girl go in for nursing in the first place? I hope,' he gave one of his laughs, 'you're not going to tell me it's because of all those glamorous doctors!'

'Goodness, no! Doctors are about the most boring people on earth!' Kate could hear the forced brightness in her voice, though Philip didn't seem to notice it. 'They're far too busy to be interesting, and besides, they *will* talk shop, which isn't really what one wants, is it? To spend an evening talking medical shop, I mean.'

'I'm very glad *you* don't want to. Do let me freshen your glass, since we're still waiting. No? You're being far too abstemious—I shall get you another one anyway!'

He went away to the bar after an annoyed look round to see if there was a waiter in evidence who could be called for an order. Kate tried not to feel like giving a sigh of relief, and then pulled herself together quickly. She was here with an extremely pleasant man, to have a good time. She glanced round the crowded bar and froze.

Nick was coming in. He looked as he had on the night of the dance, though he had his jacket on now, the pale linen setting off his broad shoulders and contrasting with the dark green of his shirt. What was he doing here, tonight of all nights?

A sharp pang of jealousy caught at her as she wondered who he was with. Surely she couldn't feel like that in the circumstances? She couldn't, after all the loathing thoughts she had had about him, be feeling this confusion of jealousy and yearning, and simply want to sit here gazing at him with the pull of attraction tearing at her . . .

He hadn't seen her, and she had just sorted out that he seemed to be with a group of four people when Philip reappeared beside her with yet another glass of whisky for himself as well as Kate's second champagne cocktail. She accepted it eagerly, giving him such a vivid smile that he seemed nonplussed for a second, then pleased. He didn't seem at all surprised when Kate gave him her riveted attention as he began to tell her all about Lincoln's Inn Fields, and his chambers there, and the chance which had brought him out here to give Lanbwe the benefit of his advice on certain aspects of its parliamentary constitution.

He couldn't know, of course, that Kate was very carefully not looking past his shoulder. She had seen that Nick was with a European couple and a Lanbwena couple, and the Lanbwena couple were Dr Jeriku and a pretty dark girl who must be his wife. The hospital was doing without two of its doctors at once, then. And no doubt Nick's date for the evening would appear any minute.

Kate became very animated, laughing appreciatively at anything Philip said which could remotely be considered funny, and fixing him with an admiring gaze which didn't seem to disconcert him at all. When a waiter appeared to usher them into the dining-room, she went on giving every evidence of enjoying herself hugely. That was because Nick and his party, still only five, came into the dining-room only a few minutes after them and sat down not far away.

The food was surprisingly good, though Kate had to remind herself not to notice the prices. She tried not to feel, too, that it was wasted on her lack of appetite. Even so, she managed to eat her way through a prawn cocktail, a rare steak with green salad, and a meringue glacé she didn't really want but which Philip insisted on ordering for her. She began to feel that Philip really did drink rather a lot—he consumed most of a bottle of wine because she laughingly put her hand over her glass regularly when he tried to fill it, and then he switched back to whisky again when the wine was finished.

And she began to wish that he wouldn't be quite so complimentary, more heavily so the more he drank, though she couldn't show it, of course, and didn't draw her hand away when he put his over it on the table. Nick, who was seated to face them, would surely notice it. His party seemed to be having a leisurely, amiable dinner. When Kate and Philip reached the coffee stage she could see that they were still chatting pleasantly over their steaks.

The casino was open now, with the doors which opened off the bar flung wide, and she agreed with every evidence of pleasure when Philip suggested smoothly that they might go and try their luck. She told herself she didn't mind, either, when Philip frowned briefly over the bill the waiter presented to him, and then made a thing out of totting it up himself on a pocket calculator before producing his credit card with bad grace.

'I'm sure you're worth it,' he murmured to her as they left the table and walked back, hand in hand, in the direction of the bar. There was a little too much meaning in his voice. Kate suddenly felt as if things had gone far enough. She wanted to look round for Nick, with the quite irrational feeling that at least he was there if things got out of hand. She crushed the thought quickly, angry with herself for so much as thinking of it. If there was one person she certainly couldn't appeal to, it was him. And she was quite capable of taking care of herself, anyway!

Since she hadn't much money with her, she'd meant to watch the roulette rather than play. Philip, however, insisted on staking her. Fortunately she won, though that didn't incline her to go on playing, and she found the intensity with which people were betting on the various different games rather off-putting. Philip decided she was bringing him luck on the roulette table and started to bet heavily. He didn't seem to mind too much when he lost, and kept slipping an arm round Kate to give her a squeeze.

She found herself aware that she didn't like Philip Hickley at all, even if he was a friend of the Barkers. She didn't know why she'd got herself into this in the first place. Drink didn't make him any less smooth, she supposed, but it did make him let out his annoying laugh more often, and he seemed to be quite manic about gambling. She wanted to go home.

'It really is time I went home!' she told Philip, trying to keep the artificial brightness in her voice. It came out almost arch, which annoyed her, and she said quickly, 'I do actually have to work tomorrow.' He couldn't know that it wasn't until the evening. 'That's what it's like for we nurses, you know!'

'Ah, but there's still tonight, isn't there?'

Oh no, there isn't, Kate thought silently, and felt relieved when he actually agreed to leave. And then she felt a faint flutter as she remembered that the house at Dendaa was empty, with Tessa away. And what was more, Philip knew Tessa was away because she'd told him so at the beginning of the evening. Still, anyone who'd drunk as much as he had surely couldn't be capable of doing much more than getting her into an embarrassing struggle . . .

'You're really quite a party-girl,' Philip said happily, as he backed the Barkers' large station-wagon out of its parking-space and veered sharply round the other cars to zoom too fast into the driveway. He placed a hand on her thigh, hot and clammy through her dress. 'Definitely a good evening, and you're going to be worth those outrageous prices they charge in there, aren't you?'

Kate decided to ignore the 'going to be', because his steering was so erratic she wasn't sure if they were going to get there at all. 'I think you'll need both hands on the wheel,' she said rapidly. 'The roads round here are really very uneven.' He did at least remove his hand, though he was still driving much too fast and kept swinging dangerously across the road. 'Are—are you sure you wouldn't rather I drove?'

'Don't be such a nervous little thing. You surely can't think I'm not capable.'

'They have a lot of traffic accidents in Lanbwe.' She wished she hadn't remembered that they did. She'd like to have said a few sharp words, too, about drunk drivers, but knew she'd better not upset his concentration on the road. 'It might be wise to go a little slower.'

'Oh no, let's get there as fast as we can. Nice empty road, nobody much about—nobody at your place either, is there?'

She thought hastily about inventing a third member of the household who just happened to be staying with them, but before she could form the lie properly another car appeared ahead of them, coming their way, and Philip so nearly steered straight into it that she almost let out a shriek.

'Bloody stupid driver—no idea of what he was doing!' Philip exclaimed, swinging round to stare back at the other car with a dangerous lack of attention, and then turning back just in time to keep the station-wagon on the road. 'Now, where's that turning? Ah, here it is. Almost home now, my dear. Pity we didn't bring another bottle of that whisky with us.'

Getting him totally incapable suddenly sounded like a very good idea to Kate, but she hadn't got any whisky anyway, and she very much hoped she was going to be able to keep him out of the house altogether. Anyway, if he got into the drive without hitting anything it would be a miracle. He did, even though she thought for a frozen moment he was going to hit the house.

'Here we are, then,' he said before she'd properly recovered from that. 'And you even left a light on to welcome us back, didn't you? There's a good girl! Hey, no need to jump out so fast, I'm coming.'

'Look,' Kate said breathlessly from the doorstep, wishing she could find her key when it seemed to have disappeared into the bottom of her bag, 'thanks for a very nice evening, but—'

'Oh, come on now! You're not going to play *that* little game!'

The door behind Kate swung open with a startling abruptness, letting out a flood of light. As she spun round—because she hadn't even found her key yet—her jaw dropped in disbelief. She'd thought, for a fraction of a second's relief, that Tessa must have come back after all. But the person who stood there, with his fair head catching the light, and looking very tall, very athletic, and very slightly threatening, was Nick.

'Ah, there you are, darling,' he said blandly. 'I wondered where you'd got to, when I came in and found you weren't here!'

Kate gulped. She was almost sure she heard Philip Hickley gulp too. Well, anyone might, faced with someone Nick's size. She certainly heard him mumble, 'Er, kind enough to entertain me on behalf of friends. I was just bringing her back. Goodnight, Kate!'

That was followed, very rapidly, by the slam of a car door. But Kate had been drawn inside by then, by an insistent, apparently affectionate hand. The door was firmly shut behind her.

'What?'

She stared up at him in bewilderment. She was too stunned to feel anything else. A car engine outside made her stir, and she said weakly, 'Oh God, I'm not sure he's fit to drive!'

'Lucky you got here at all then, and aren't lying in a mangled heap at the side of the road waiting for some poor doctor to put you back together again.' Nick sounded trenchantly unsympathetic. 'I thought he was too far gone to have noticed me at the Inn, and he was, wasn't he?'

'How did you? Why did you—'

'Why is a very good one. How, if you mean how did I get in, is through the door. With a key. One Tessa lent me once, and I seem to have forgotten to return.'

That should have sparked some response in her, but she was still too dazed at the sight of him. She felt a sudden aching longing to forget everything except his nearness and a desire to collapse into the nearest chair, though she stayed on her feet instead. She blinked up at him, trying to pull herself together.

'Are you rescuing me again, by any chance?'

'That was the idea. It was pretty obvious what you might get into.' He gave her a level, unsmiling look. 'I don't,' he said softly, dangerously, 'need your thanks, though I'm sure you weren't going to offer them to me.'

The electricity between them in the small room was suddenly as strong as the storms of a few days ago had been. Kate almost expected to feel her hair crackle, and hear the crash of thunder overhead. She couldn't move, and didn't want to. She was mesmerised by the smoky grey eyes fixed on hers; by the long, dynamic length of him; by the tanned, slightly roughened skin and mobile mouth and firm jaw and the masculine strength of him poised so close to her. When his hands began to come out towards her it seemed to be happening in slow motion . . .

But if he touched her she would be lost. No matter what his motives were, no matter how much she knew it was calculation. With that knowledge, and with the need to protect herself from her own weak longing to be in his arms no matter what, she felt a sharp, stabbing desire to hurt him—to cut at him as deeply as he had cut her. And if she didn't have the physical strength to keep him off, at least she had her tongue.

'Oh, for goodness' sake, Cousin Nick, don't start that again! I know some girl jilted you, and married your best friend or something, but I really am sick of being grabbed just because you're neurotic enough to need to prove yourself! Twice is enough!'

His eyes had gone as blank as if she had slapped him. At that moment she wanted to take it all back, every word, but he had dropped his hands. And then he walked past her, avoiding any contact, so that she felt as if she had been brushed aside like a gnat.

The door shut and he was gone. Just like that. Kate stared at the closed door, and wanted to burst into tears.

CHAPTER NINE

THOUGHTS which wouldn't go away kept her awake, and haunted her all through the next day, too.

He would never forgive her for flinging the girl he loved in his face. For reminding him . . . But of course, he had never forgotten anyway.

She ought not to want him to forgive her. There was no way of deceiving herself that things could be different between them—that it would all turn out to be a bad dream and she could put the clock back to not knowing.

Besides, even if he had loved *her*, instead of the girl in the photograph, and even if all the business over Tessa had simply never happened, it still couldn't have led anywhere. He came from a close family who would certainly never accept her. She had a parent who would certainly fall into hysterics at the thought of *him*!

There was no point in thinking about that, anyway, because it was simply sliding into fantasy.

Kate went on duty heavy-eyed, and for once with a feeling of dread, and then spent four nights running an unnaturally quiet Unit, with absolutely no need to call in a doctor at all. And nobody came round, either. If it hadn't been for the sight of Nick's signature scribbled on various patients' notes she would have thought he had vanished from the hospital entirely. She trailed on and off duty, and kept away from the Barkers in case Philip Hickley was still there until she met Sally, and learned that he had flown back to England already.

Everything seemed suddenly empty. She started playing with the idea of resigning, quitting the Mutala job and asking to be flown back to London. She wouldn't be the same person if she went back, because she knew she had changed. It was more than just Africa that had changed her, though she had the feeling that Africa was part of it. Surely it must change anyone to come out to this huge continent with its stark contrasts of the primitive and the civilised, its extremes of wealth and poverty, its sense of spaciousness going on for thousands and thousands of miles of unbroken land? Part of her didn't want to leave, but to go on living with the sense of challenge she had found here. Besides, she still had almost eight months of her contract to run, and she didn't belong anywhere else—certainly not back at St John's with the ghost of her old self. But could she really go on working here?

She was still thinking about it when she went back on day duty, reporting for the one o'clock shift and then setting about the afternoon's routines. There was no delivery in progress so she went to see to the babies, finding herself with an extra urge to give the day-old infants a cuddle as she picked them up to weigh and change them after their lunch-time feed. There was always a sense of comfort in the way any baby would snuggle instinctively against a warm shoulder. Kate was putting the last of them down when Sister Labatsu appeared round the partition, looking hurried.

'Ah, Staff Nurse, there you are! You don't mind flying, do you? It doesn't make you sick or anything?'

'No, Sister, I don't get travel-sick at all.' The unexpectedness of the question had made Kate jump. Flying? Could Sister suddenly read minds and know that she had been wondering whether to leave or not?

'Good, I shall send you, then. Would you get the emergency equipment together and be ready to drive yourself out to the airfield? We've got one of our occasional air call-outs. The village clinic at Tiflak can't cope with this one, and it must be a thoroughly experienced midwife who goes, just in case you have to cope with all sorts of things on the way back. Come along now, we've already alerted the Emergency Air Service, and there'll be a light plane and pilot waiting at the airfield for you.'

Kate was already moving, everything else forgotten. A thread of excitement ran through her veins. This really was something new, and a challenge too. She hoped she could rise to it.

The plane looked tiny when Kate reached it. She'd known it would be small, because Sister had explained that there would only be room for her, her stretcher-case, and the pilot, on the journey back. But it was still a shock to see it looking like a toy, with its bright green and white paint. Her heart gave a little lurch, but she hurried across to where it stood waiting.

She had the standard delivery pack with her, and an extra pack of drugs, in this case pethilorfan and phenergan with plastic syringes with which to administer them. She had drip equipment too, though Tiflak Clinic would have some of its own, and anything else she might need too. It was apparently quite well-equipped within its limits, though it had no theatre or proper surgical facilities, so that the girl who was in obstructed labour would have to be brought back to Mutala for a Caesarean. The radio message had come from the local police post and had suggested that the patient could be moved. A three-hundred-mile journey before a Caesarean should prove feasible. Kate hoped so, because apart from one nurse and two orderlies stationed at Tiflak, she would be on her own.

'Hallo, Nurse! Stas Novak at your service.' The pilot had straightened up at her approach, and was giving her a cheerful grin. 'Flown in a Cessna before? Don't worry, *I* do it all the time!'

He had light brown hair and a small moustache, and his slight accent, together with the name, suggested that he might be Polish. He showed her where to stow her gear and explained cheerfully that the second seat would be taken out when they got there to accommodate the stretcher. It looked as if it would be very cramped, but his attitude suggested that it was just an everyday job to him, which was comforting.

Besides, the plane must be more solid than it looked, Kate thought with a tremor of nerves, even if it did look horribly like an enlarged version of one of those models made of balsa wood. Anyway, she'd got to fly in it, so there was no use worrying.

'When we get there, could you try and make a decision fairly quickly?' the pilot asked easily, giving her his grin again. 'It'd be better if we could come back by daylight. Not that I couldn't fly this crate in the dark, but getting back in the light would be better! Just sit yourself in there and clip the belt on. Oh, hang on a minute.'

Someone was calling him, and he walked away to meet a running uniformed figure who stopped to talk to him urgently. A moment later he was back. 'Sorry, we've got to wait for another passenger,' he said. 'Not for long, I hope. Get settled anyway, and I'll get the engine revved up while we wait.'

It was noisy, sitting in the small plane while the engine coughed and then settled down to a steady roar. The pilot was murmuring into his radio, apparently giving a flight-plan and checking on their departure. Kate made sure all over again that she was strapped in, and looked round. She'd never visualised herself as part of a flying-nurse service. She wondered about the condition of the patient she was to fetch. There wasn't much room, if she found herself delivering a baby in mid-air, so if flying set off normal labour after all, she would have quite a job to manage things.

The plane's door was pulled open, and a lean figure ducked in. Kate was bemused to see who it was, and then extraordinarily relieved, as Nick, none other, tapped the pilot on the shoulder and shouted that he was here. Kate forgot everything, and shouted herself, above the engine noise, as he folded into the second seat and fumbled for the strap. The pilot began at once to taxi down the air-strip.

'They've sent you too? Oh, that's good.'

'Sorry, different emergency. If they'd only get their messages co-ordinated we could have saved time by driving to the airfield together.'

There didn't seem to be any chance to say more, as the pilot began to turn the plane and then picked up speed on the empty runway. By the time Kate had gulped a little and nerved herself for leaving the ground, she had begun to remember that Nick wasn't someone she wanted to see. Except as a doctor, when he would have been both useful and reassuring . . .

She glanced at him, sitting calm and apparently unmoved in the other seat, far too near at hand, and felt a prickle of hostility. Why did it have to be him, if he wasn't even going to be useful on her case? She found all at once that they had left the ground without her noticing, and were climbing steadily into a sky of Lanbwe's usual vivid blue, though it looked much whiter from up here.

'What's *your* emergency, then?' she asked him coldly, raising her voice enough to reach him across the engine's now-steadier roar.

'I'm going further north than you. Accident, up in the bush area.' He gave her a coolly impersonal look. 'I'm sure you'll manage without me!'

A cold feeling of misery welled inside her. She turned her shoulder to peer out of the small window, determined to look as if she wasn't aware of anything except the scenery below, which was spreading out now in its pattern of flatness and scrub and dry yellow dust. She certainly didn't want to be aware that he was so close, shut up with her in this small box of a plane. She didn't want to feel an almost automatic tingling in the arm nearest to him. They were both at work, even here, and even if neither of them wanted to see each other, that was the way it had to be.

'We'll be flying over South Africa in a moment. Shortest route,' Nick's voice said. He still sounded impersonal. 'Heading north-west. Look out for the river, if you want to be able to see where we are.'

She could have asked his advice about her case, Kate realised a few moments later, except that she didn't know more than the bare details of it. But, on the other hand, she wasn't going to have him thinking she couldn't cope with it by herself when she was obviously supposed to.

His touch on her arm made her jump, but when she looked round angrily he merely pointed out and down. 'River,' he told her, 'and if you look hard enough you may even see some wildlife around it. Some kinds of deer, anyway, and you might even catch sight of a hippo.'

There was more greenery below now, and the narrow meandering line of water. She caught a glimpse of a small herd of something just moving in under the trees. The grinding noise of the plane's engine was beginning to make her ears ache.

Nick looked relaxed and easy, his head turned half way to look out of his side of the plane. Kate bit her lip and hastily turned away again in case he should catch her watching him. She made herself concentrate on the landscape again, and on thinking what she would find when she reached her destination. A small clinic and a young girl in obstructed labour. A stretcher to bring her home on. A local nurse in charge of the clinic. She must be a trained midwife if she was a Lanbwena nurse, but she didn't think this case could be managed by a forceps delivery, obviously, or she wouldn't have sent out an emergency call. It was a first baby and a very young mother, that much Kate had been told, and the hitch in the labour didn't seem to have any added complications like fever or toxaemia or prematurity.

The pilot looked round to see that they were all right, gave a cheerful thumbs-up sign which Nick answered, and went back to concentrating on flying the plane. It didn't really feel unsafe, now that they were up in the air, and his easy manner gave a feeling of confidence. They ground on steadily, and Kate couldn't help feeling that they must look like a gnat from below, buzzing across the blue sky far above.

They began to lose height at last, slowly. Kate was beginning to be tired of the unnatural silence between herself and Nick, though she told herself that she wasn't going to break it. She didn't want to talk to him to try to revive that friendship which had existed before, where she could have asked him things and got a friendly and knowledgeable answer. She couldn't feel an ordinary friendship towards him now, anyway, because even sitting beside him sent her into a quivery awareness and filled her with uncertainty. The memory of his touch mocked her.

The pilot was murmuring into his radio again now, and as they sank still lower, Kate caught sight of buildings ahead. First there was something with a red cross painted on the top of it, set among a small group of trees. That must be Tiflak Clinic. They were approaching an air-strip now, and Kate set her teeth for a landing. Abruptly, however, the pilot zoomed in low and rose again, making her stomach give a flip.

'Damn blasted donkeys,' he shouted over his shoulder, 'all over the runway again! I always have to buzz 'em before I can land!' Then he was coming back in again, though he was still talking cheerfully to his passengers, making Kate wish he would give his whole attention to getting them down safely. 'I can see your two Land Rovers waiting, so they seem to be on the ball all right. You aren't expecting to come back with us, are you, Doc? Haven't been told to wait for you, anyway, and—'

'I'll get another plane back later,' Nick called. 'The police have it in hand.'

'OK. I was going to say that we wouldn't have room for you both with a stretcher-case in, so I hoped some-body'd thought of that!' The pilot was landing even as he spoke, the wheels touching down neatly with only the barest bump.

Kate tried not to look at Nick as they drew to a halt and she undid the strap which held her. Now she had to pull herself together and concentrate on nothing but her patient, hoping that she wouldn't find things had got worse since the radio message.

Nick was on the door side, so he jumped out first, the bag he had brought with him in his hand. He reached up civilly to help Kate, and she had to let him. As he steadied her, his hands warm against her arms, she could almost swear that he held her a little bit too long, and her defensive glance upward showed a gleam in his eyes.

'Good luck with your case. I've got to go another seventy miles, so I'd better be off.'

Then he was away at a fast lope towards the Land Rovers she could see parked a little way off beside the runway, forgetting her entirely, she was bitterly sure, as soon as his back was turned on her. He jumped into the one with the police driver and they were off at once in a whirl of dust. She had to resist the temptation to stare after him.

She didn't have time to stand still. 'There's yours,' the pilot was saying, pointing at the other Land Rover. 'I'll help you take the gear over. Then I'll get that second seat taken out. Oh, Nurse, try and remember what I said, will you? About the light? I know you can't always help it, but if you have a choice, try not to be more than, say, two hours, will you?'

Kate nodded. 'Have you got oxygen in the plane, in case I need it coming back?' she asked him quickly.

'Yes. And we can keep a drip steady if you need one, by tying it to a strut. I'll get the police to radio back and tell your hospital we've arrived.'

Her Land Rover had an orderly driving, a dark Lanbwena in a white jacket. He must be one of the paramedics who were given basic training and then sent out to the outlying clinics to deal with everything from cuts to simple fractures, to teach hygiene, and to give penicillin and anti-tetanus injections. He told Kate that the patient was much the same, but Sister was glad she had come so quickly. Sometimes it took a lot longer if all the emergency planes were out doing something else.

They were soon drawing to a halt outside the small clinic building, which was square and white-painted and set among a scattering of dried-up thorn trees. Even up here they seemed to flourish better than the other vegetation, spreading their spindly black branches sideways and pointing dagger-like thorns at the sky. Sister came to meet them at the clinic door, and turned out to be a round, energetic, middle-aged lady wearing a State Enrolled Nurse's badge.

'We've got Nanda sedated,' she told Kate as she led her in, not wasting any time. 'She came to us from her local clinic, twenty miles away, after she'd been in labour for forty-eight hours without making any progress. We've got more facilities here so we got the police to bring her in.'

'How long ago was that?'

'Yesterday, twenty-four hours ago now. She was perfectly healthy ante-natally, and she did attend the clinic regularly too.'

'How old is she?' Kate asked.

'Sixteen. She was baptised by one of the missionaries, so we know that exactly,' Sister said. 'No reason at all why she shouldn't make a good primogeniture. She's a good little girl, and hasn't been fussing at all, but she's been having rather a bad time!'

She took Kate into a tiny room which was bare except for a bed and one chair. The whole clinic was so small that Kate was a little surprised to hear that this place had more facilities than somewhere else. The bed was a standard hospital one, with a white coverlet on it drawn up over a very young, dark-skinned girl with beads of sweat glinting on her forehead. A dextrose drip was set up beside the bed with a tube leading down to the girl's arm.

'Nanda,' Sister said gently as the girl turned dull eyes towards them, the pupils showing signs of her sedation. Then the older nurse turned back to Kate.

'It's no use trying to explain things to her because she only speaks her own local dialect. I have a few words of it, but not very many. If you sign to her what you want to do, though, she's very co-operative. We've had her on a drip, of course, ever since she arrived. I've seen the baby's head once, but she just doesn't seem to be able to push it out!'

Her eyes showed her kindly concern for the girl, and she held the young hand in hers for a moment while Kate paused for an initial assessment before she made an examination. Nanda's skin looked healthy and there was no greenish tinge in it. No puffiness either, to suggest toxaemia, and although she was breathing shallowly there was no faint rattle. The whites of her eyes were clear. Kate took her pulse and felt it steady, if a little fast, but she wanted to be sure, before she took the girl on a plane, that she wasn't going to deliver en route.

'Nanda? I'm just going to have a look at you.' She knew the girl couldn't understand her, but she thought her voice would give reassurance as she turned the coverlet gently back. 'Could you pass me the disposable gloves in that packet there, please, Sister?'

Kate made her examination, and then straightened up thoughtfully. 'I can't see any sign of the head at the moment. How was it when you saw it?'

'Normal, certainly correctly positioned. Ah, she's pushing again!'

The girl let out a soft groan, her teeth biting against her lips. Kate bent again quickly, with a swift smile of encouragement. This time, she too saw the head, just a part of it, and she could see the way the skull was distorting just a little. A baby's head was fairly mobile but it shouldn't be allowed to crush too much. The head disappeared again abruptly as Nanda panted. It seemed she couldn't get any further.

'Caput and moulding,' Kate said, frowning a little. 'She looks a little far on to move, don't you think? Had you thought of using forceps, Sister?'

'Well now, there's a problem. I haven't actually got any. We could try it, if you brought some with you?'

'No.' They didn't put them in the delivery pack. Only artery forceps and two pairs of scissors. Kate hadn't thought of adding delivery forceps for the trip, and neither had Sister Labatsu, believing that Tiflak Clinic was well equipped. 'You haven't got *any*?' Kate repeated, startled.

'I did have, but they've gone missing. The second pair were broken and sent down for repairs on a plane a few weeks ago. I don't like doing forceps deliveries anyway when I can avoid them. Too much risk of tearing, and we aren't equipped to repair properly afterwards without sending a girl down to the hospital.'

'No, I can see your point.' Kate bit her lip. She felt a sudden longing for Nick's advice, but he was miles away by now. To wait or not to wait? If this baby could possibly be delivered here, it would seem a better risk than having it suddenly arrive on the plane. If that should happen and be followed by haemorrhage, they might have a very nasty situation indeed.

At that moment Nanda started pushing again, and Kate made encouraging noises, and bent over to study the situation again. Surely the head was a little further out this time?

She decided that they *had* to wait for a little while, with the girl coming so near to progress and not looking as if she had exhausted her capacities yet. Kate monitored the foetal heart and found it strong and steady. She and Sister between them tried changing the girl's position to see if lying on her side would make it easier for her to push. A squat might have been even better, but they couldn't move the girl by force, and it was hard to make her understand anything very much. After an hour, they still hadn't got any further, and Kate was beginning to sense a slight irregularity in the foetal heart-beat too, though it was still strong. Nanda was tired, but still trying hard, with such patience that Kate felt for her. It was no use, they would have to risk the journey.

Forty-five minutes on the plane—it wasn't long. A short drive from here on a stretcher, the flight, an ambulance to whisk them back to Mutala hospital . . . It was going to be the only thing to do, risk or no risk.

She made up her mind and set about her preparations. The pethilorfan and phenergan injection should help, and she gave it while Sister soothed the young girl gently and the orderly came in to strap her on to a stretcher. Sister came with them to see Nanda on to the plane, and it only seemed a few moments then before the stretcher was loaded into the space where the second seat had been. Kate crouched down beside it, holding up the drip while the pilot tied the dextrose bottle firmly onto the nearest strut with a piece of bandage.

'Makeshift but effective,' he said cheerfully. 'Poor kid. Not very old, is she? They start young round here. Going to stay right next to her, Nurse? You might find it a bit bumpy, but I'll try to make it a gentle take-off.'

'I'll have to. I'm going to have to monitor her all the

way.' Kate was praying that she hadn't left it too late, in her attempt to do the best thing. Sister had seemed to agree with her, but had been all too happy to leave the decision to her.

'Can we set up the oxygen for her, please?' Kate asked, with a calm she was far from feeling.

The pilot dealt with that, his neat movements showing long practice. Kate let Nanda take a gulp from the mask, soothing her gently with her hand as she made another quick check on the foetal heart. All right so far. All right all the way, she prayed, and if she had to go to a distant village clinic again, she'd take delivery forceps with her and no mistake. Then the plane door was shut, and pilot was climbing into his seat, the engine was revving up. The sympathetic faces which had been surrounding them were gone, and it was all up to Kate, the pilot, and Nanda now.

She wasn't afraid of flying in the small plane this time. She was much more afraid of having to do a mid-air delivery. She had to stop Nanda pushing, which was difficult when the girl didn't know what she was saying. The best she could do was make shushing noises and shake her head, holding the girl's hand sympathetically and laying her other hand against the girl's abdomen.

She saw the baby's head again twice. It didn't seem to be any more moulded, which was a good thing anyway, and it seemed very determined to stay alive. Kate was determined it should, too. She wasn't going to lose this baby. And neither was Nanda, so patient and quiet with no more than a few bitten-back groans to show the long pain she was going through. She seemed to trust Kate, and perhaps after all she had been through so far, she barely noticed that she was flying high in the air above her country. She was lying still and having one of her inert spells when Kate heard static crackle near to her and realised suddenly that the pilot had turned round to hand her a pair of earphones.

'For you, on the radio-phone,' he said clearly. 'They want a report on your patient's condition. The mike is there, attached.'

Kate managed to fumble herself into the earphones and gave a rapid description of Nanda's current condition and a brief summing-up of the past hours. The voice which was questioning her came over faintly distorted, and she felt unreal, sitting here giving a status report from the inside of the tiny plane. They told her, though, that an ambulance would be standing by for them at the airfield. It wouldn't be long now.

She was scarcely aware of the gradual sinking of the plane, for she was busy monitoring the foetal heart and worrying about the tiny breaks in the beat as it ticked in her ear. Nanda stirred and moaned and clutched at the oxygen mask again. At least she wasn't pushing, though. She seemed, at last, too tired to make herself worse by doing that. Kate was grateful for the pilot's skill, and the way he had seemed to be able to make the ride somehow smoother than before. She was even more grateful when she was suddenly aware of the very softest of bumps, and realised all at once that they were actually down. They'd made it, and this baby was going to reach the hospital in time, and get itself born by Caesarean section, with everything needed to resuscitate it if necessary and a nice warm incubator to lie in afterwards . . .

The ambulance was waiting, pulled up with its doors open. Sister Labatsu was there too, surprisingly, primed with Kate's report and ready to make a check herself. They sped back along the road and Sister didn't object when Kate said she'd like to go into theatre and see the job through. Mr Olinga was there to operate and there was an amazing air of efficiency, considering this was Mutala Hospital, with all its shortages and problems and general air of improvised coping.

'Well, Staff Nurse, that's one very fine baby boy,

Sister told her later, beaming. 'We don't even need to put him in an incubator, do we? Far too big a lad for that—all of eight pounds, and strong and healthy!' She looked almost as proud of him as Kate felt. 'The mother doesn't seem the worse for it all, either, does she? She's just coming round. Go and show her you're here, so that she can see a familiar face. And try and tell her I'll bring the baby for her to see in a moment.'

It was actually over. Kate could scarcely believe it. There were only the notes to write out now. Pages of them, she realised with a weary grimace. But everything had to be written down and signed, and she only remembered when she was in the middle of doing them that she hadn't had a chance to thank the pilot, because they'd all rushed away so fast on arrival. He'd certainly done his job, and so had she, thanks to his expert flying.

She only remembered Nick then, too, the thought of him coming back to her with a muted stab. Where was he now? Somewhere a long way up-country still. They had flown half-way across Lanbwe together, and he was still out there, dealing with his own emergency. She wished he was here and that she could share her triumph with him.

Sister told her that she could stay off duty tomorrow instead of coming in for the afternoon shift, because she had worked extra hours tonight. Kate was surprised to see it was so late and was feeling so happy with her relief that she would almost have hung around in the Unit, if Sister hadn't shooed her away in a motherly fashion.

'It's lucky you didn't have to go any further north than Tiflak. I heard on the police radio that there's guerrilla activity up there. A party of them from across the border trying to fight it out with the Security Forces,' Rose, who had just come in for the night, said.

'Hush, Staff Nurse, don't gossip,' Sister said reprovingly. 'It's probably just a rumour anyway. You know how these things go round.'

'No, Sister,' Rose insisted. 'I heard it on my cousin's set just before I came on duty.'

'How much further north than Tiflak?' Kate found herself asking suddenly, and with a sharp memory. Hadn't Nick said he was going north?

'About forty kilometres,' Rose said, but Sister was hushing her again, firmly.

'We won't talk about that now, and Nurse Raven's going off duty. Run along, Staff Nurse. And well done, you dealt with that very well indeed!'

Kate could only go, in the face of Sister's insistence. Her mind was struggling to make the conversion between miles and kilometres, and failing. She had never managed to feel anything but muddled about it. But what kind of accident had Nick gone to? Would he be in danger? Would he find himself in the middle of people firing indiscrimately or get himself captured?

She shouldn't have cared whether he got shot or not. It should have been a matter of complete indifference to her. It certainly shouldn't have kept her awake half the night, waking and sleeping and waking again. Nor should it have been a matter for urgent prayers, childish ones.

He would be back at the hospital in the morning; he *would*—as odious as ever, as untrustworthy, as inclined to play with other people's feelings.

He *would* be safe—surely?

CHAPTER TEN

SHE RANG Maternity in the morning, on the excuse of asking how Nanda and the baby were. Timing it carefully, she had hoped to speak to Rose—but Rose was busy, and she could hardly ask casual questions of a trainee about whether anybody had heard if Dr Kyle had got back yet. Besides, if he had, someone might tell him she'd asked.

She mooched about the house for a while, trying to talk sense into herself, then made herself eat some breakfast which she didn't want. Then she sat down and tried to read a book before she had a burst of activity and decided to clean the house up thoroughly. She kept glancing at the phone, though she knew nobody was likely to ring her, and wanting to drive to the hospital.

She had to go out in the end, because she couldn't stay indoors any longer. It was the usual dry sixty-five degrees, summery to Kate, winter to any Lanbwena, and the wind hadn't got up for once. She put on shorts and a shirt and picked up a cardigan, deciding suddenly to go out to the Dam. It would be empty there. The Lanbwena never seemed to bother to go there, and the expatriate families only went at weekends and holiday times. Kate began to coil up her hair to get it out of the way, then in the end left it hanging in a single plait down her back.

Reaching into the pocket of the uniform dress she had taken off yesterday in search of an elastic band, she found, as well, the post she had picked up on her way on duty yesterday and had then forgotten about. There were two for Tessa and one for Kate from her mother, though she had felt, yesterday, guiltily disinclined to open it. Somehow she felt even more disinclined now, casting a glance at her father's photograph, which stood propped up on her dressing-table, but reproached herself, sighed, and decided to take it with her.

She went out, and saw Penny Sinclair pinning up washing in the next door garden. Penny gave her a wave and called out to invite her in for lunch, but Kate called back that she was going to the Dam for some fresh air, trying not to look as disinclined as she felt for company.

'Take our canoe out if you want to!' Penny called back. 'Ask the man at the boathouse for our key. Say I said you could have it!'

Kate gave her another wave in thanks, though she knew, as she drove off along the Dam road, that she didn't feel like boating. Sculling around in a canoe was too placid an occupation for the way she was feeling. But at least it was a comfort to see water, she thought, as she parked her car and decided she'd walk along beside the large artificial lake. After all these months in Lanbwe without a single drop of rain, even the idea of water lying open and free in a wide expanse like this seemed strange, let alone the memory of London drizzle. It hadn't rained since she'd been here, and it wouldn't until September, unless there was some freak weather.

She decided to open her mother's letter now, and then leave it in the car while she went for her walk, since she hadn't a pocket in her shorts large enough to stuff it in. And, no, she wouldn't be unwilling to read it. The thought gave her a nasty stab of disloyalty.

Tearing it open and starting to skim through the contents, she was glad, if a little surprised, to see that her mother seemed much more cheerful than usual. And then discovered why, as she turned the page and read that Mrs Raven had decided to get married again.

To a colonel she had met playing bridge. Such a charming man, in his sixties. She seemed to be trying to break it to Kate gently . . .

Well, Kate thought numbly, it was nice. She'd be able to write back and say how glad she was. It was ironic to know that her mother seemed to think she'd mind, for she certainly didn't.

Tessa getting married, perhaps even married by now, depending how long that took in South Africa. And her mother getting married. Everybody seemed to be sorting themselves out satisfactorily into pairs, didn't they?

Kate put the letter in her car, locked up, and walked off along the lake. If she kept her mind on it, she could think about nothing but the scenery. The lake showed it was the dry season, with a rim of yellow mud at its edges and no sign of movement, as if the river which was supposed to feed it had dried up altogether. It probably had. She walked absently along the banks, watching the diving birds which lived here. Lanbwe didn't seem to have many birds besides these. She was trying to make herself think about them because that was better than thinking about Nick.

She walked quite a way and then turned back. It didn't seem to be doing her any good being out here. She mooched along, keeping her eyes on the ground, telling herself that she was looking for insect life. That was better than thinking. She was almost back to the car when she glanced up—and then it was almost as if a sudden awareness had made her look. There was another car parked beside hers now, but she didn't look at that, because her eyes had flown to the figure who stood waiting for her. Very obviously waiting for her, since he was quite deliberately leaning against her car.

Relief that he was safe must have shown in Kate's face, because she was only three yards away and the grey eyes were watching her intently. Idiotically, she wanted to reach out to him. But she was furious with him, wasn't she? She turned away sharply, but his voice called her back.

'That first expression was better. And there's no point in going anywhere, because I'm going to go on standing guard over your car until you talk to me!'

'Did your trip go well?' she asked quickly, with icy politeness, swinging back to face him. 'Your emergency, I mean?'

'No, not very, as a matter of fact. It isn't easy to have to recommend an amputation. But we aren't going to talk about that.' He was eyeing her thoughtfully and her heart gave an uneven thump to see him standing there so tall and fair, so much *Nick* that it brought a painful dryness into her throat. 'When I got back this morning,' he went on.

'Oh yes?'

'Will you listen? The way you're looking at me, you might as well have your fingers in your ears!' He sounded rough and exasperated all at once, and took a step towards her. When she flinched back he looked more exasperated than ever, but she saw him rein himself in deliberately. 'The other night you showed what a nasty tongue you have on you, Cousin Kate. And if I weren't so ridiculously in love with you, I wouldn't be here.'

That was too much, stinging her like a goad. 'You can stop all the pretence,' Kate flashed, against a throb of hurt. She was too angry to care, or to mind her words. 'You can stop trying, however boring it must have been for you! Tessa's safely married by now, or about to be! Let alone that you'd got it all wrong in the first place. Richard was never interested in me, which is something I'm all too glad about. And *you're* just—a—'

'Stop it.' His hands came out and caught hold of her wrists. When she would have pulled them away she couldn't, firmly held by his fingers. 'Stop it, Kate, and stop tying yourself up in misunderstandings. Do you hear me?' He added with a touch of grimness, 'Don't say things we both might regret—please?'

'You don't have to address me as if I was a hysterical child!'

'No. And you'd have every right to be angry if what you'd thought was true. It isn't. And, good God,' he said, in a tone of rueful exasperation, 'if I'd known that a light-hearted and supposedly comforting joke was going to come up out of the past and cause all this confusion, I'd never have made it in the first place! Oh yes, I know what Tessa said to you! I managed to elicit it, after hearing the rest of her good news, in a phone call she made to me from Johannesburg just after I got back this morning. And then, of course, I came hunting for you.' He paused, and added pointedly, 'And I know now that you'd got some crazy idea about Tessa being in love with me, until just the other night. It did explain one or two things. You really did think I was carrying on, didn't you?'

'Well, you—I—'

'You were keeping away from me as firmly as if I had the plague. Brushing me off with all that light friendliness alternating with a freeze. Oh yes, love, I did notice.' The 'love' was said deliberately, so deliberately that it seemed to send a deep tremor through every fibre of Kate's being. 'I do know that you're not the trusting type when it comes to men, and I know why, remember?'

'Don't you dare start being kind to me,' Kate managed on a ragged breath, and with a wave of hurt resentment sweeping back to make her flash him a glare and try to draw her hands away. He wouldn't let her, but held them fast.

'*Kind*? Don't be such an idiot, I want to shake you!' That was abrasive enough to sound more like the Nick she knew and the grip he had on her wrists was hard

enough to hurt, too. As if he realised it, he loosened
his fingers a little, though not enough to let her escape.
'I don't,' he said grimly, 'go round being *kind* to girls
I've fallen in love with against my better judgment.
And I don't go round grabbing people, either, unless
they just happen to turn me on so much that I can't
help myself.'

'You're still in love with—with whoever-she-is,' Kate
brought out swiftly.

'No I'm not. Oh, I *was*. There was a certain amount
of truth in it when I told Tessa about it. *Then*.' He gave
Kate's wrists a little shake as if he had to emphasise it,
looking down at her with a rueful, exasperated patience
which had something else in it too. A glint of humour,
a touch of self-mockery, and a warmth in the eyes which
never left her face, so that something inside her was
starting to thaw, suddenly, into a flood of disbelieving
happiness.

'All right,' he said, 'I'll tell you about Amy, shall I?
Since you seem to want to know and, I hope, for all the
right reasons. Amy and I were inseparable from when
I was seventeen. And yes, I was hurt and furious when,
instead of getting round to marrying me, she upped and
married one of my closest friends instead. I even did all
the right things. Chucked up my job, came away to
Africa, nursed a so-called broken heart and a lot of
bruised pride. And, yes, it did take me a long time to
get around to acknowledging that she was right in what
she'd said—that we were just used to each other. That
if we'd really been still in love we'd have got married
instead of endlessly putting if off, waiting for this, waiting for that, long after we'd both qualified. She's a
doctor, by the way, so we went through medical school
together as well as everything else. But she *was* right.
And for a while now I've been able to see that she was.
Particularly,' he said pointedly, 'lately.'

'You still keep her picture!'

'Yes, angel, but didn't it occur to you that I didn't even know where I'd put it? *Angel*,' he said on a sudden snort, and drawing her against him with a gleam in his eyes. 'More like a *demon*, a thorn in my side!'

'Nick . . .'

'Yes, darling? Can we go back to the beginning, where I was telling you I was ridiculously in love with you and hoping that we might get over all this fighting and mistaken-identity stuff? You do love me, don't you? *Don't you*?' he asked insistently, with his lips so close to hers that she wanted to melt against him and be kissed. 'You couldn't have looked at me as you did today, when you first saw me, otherwise—could you? Or have sounded jealous? *Could* you?'

'I love you,' Kate said faintly, obediently. And then at the last minute turned her face away against his neck, because a sob was coming up into her throat. She was incredibly, unbearably happy, so she shouldn't be crying. She was caught up safe and warm in his arms and he *loved* her. But the last few days had just been too much.

'Kate? What's the matter?'

'I'm just so glad you didn't get sh-shot—'

'Shot? Who was going to shoot me? Except you, if somebody had been rash enough to give you a gun!'

'Rose said there was trouble up there. Where you went. And I was worried about you,' Kate said on a gulp, but trying to turn it into a smile. A tremulous but loving smile, because he had drawn back a little to look at her. She was foolishly, idiotically, thoughtlessly happy, so that she could say almost with exasperation, 'I was scared stiff, if you want to know!'

'Oh, so that's what made you melt! Thank goodness for lucky chances! No, I didn't see any of that. The police mentioned something, but we didn't run into any of it. Did you think I might have gone up there to take bullets out of people?' He was drawing her close again, his arms sliding round her to pull her against him. He said, softly but with a touch of mischief, 'So you were scared for me even though you hated my guts? That's good.'

He did kiss her then, hard and sweet and full of delight, making her blood race with a willing joy. When he lifted his head at last they were both breathless and there was a dark, smoky light in his eyes which made her feel even weaker at the knees than ever. If that were possible. He said, huskily but with a laugh in it, 'You do pack a punch, my love, do you know that? And for the record, I am *not* trying to prove anything, except perhaps to you.'

'I'm sorry. I shouldn't have said that.'

'Considering what you thought, I'm surprised it wasn't worse. But did you really have to make such an appalling reading of my character?' His lips brushed the tip of her nose in a tiny, mocking kiss. 'And after I'd saved you from your drunken escort, too. Who was he, by the way?'

'Oh—just a very temporary acquaintance!'

'Good, because I can get just as jealous as you can. In fact that's probably why I was there at all. It certainly wasn't mere cousinly concern. Let's follow Tess and Richard's example, shall we? I'll only forgive you for your abysmal view of me if you'll marry me!'

'Nick—'

'I mean it, Kate,' he told her, his voice taking on a sudden command as if he saw the doubt in her face. 'It's marriage or nothing. I know what you're going to say, but you've got to learn to trust.'

'It's not that!' She was on the edge of tears again suddenly. It was like coming down from heaven too fast to have to remember. 'You can't marry me. Your family must hate me!'

'Nonsense. My parents would never take sides in someone else's fight—unlike me,' he added with sudden ruefulness, and then went on quickly. 'They wouldn't even think of it, and neither would any of the rest, so you can put that out of your head once and for all. As for Norma, she would always have welcomed you for David's sake, and she certainly hasn't changed. I know that because,' he gave her a faintly wary look for a second, 'I wrote and told her I'd met you. And she wrote back and told me to be particularly nice to you. See? Though if you're now going to think I've only fallen in love with you to please my *aunt*—'

'No,' she said quickly, because the look of loving exasperation he was giving her threatened to overwhelm her entirely. 'Did—did she really say that?'

'She did. She also said she'd got a locket of your grandmother's which she knew David always wanted you to have, and should she send it? I was going to raise that with you later, if I could ever get near you!' His arms tightened round her as if to prove that he had, but he was going on swiftly, with a tiny frown. 'I know your mother's going to be a problem, but I've been thinking about that. I know it seems difficult, and you're going to worry about upsetting her, but we can't live our lives through another generation, can we? Not over something this important?'

'N-no—but—'

'It's a problem as old as time. And I'm blowed if I'm going to play Romeo and Juliet, and die dramatically across your tomb!'

He sounded so explosive, and so determined, that Kate wanted to laugh. 'But I was going to say,' she told him, 'that since my mother's decided to marry a bridge-playing colonel, perhaps she won't be quite so—perhaps she won't—'

'That might occupy her thoughts a bit, might it? And besides, if we get married out here, she'll have time to get used to it, won't she?'

He was making it sound extraordinarily simple. And

possible. Whether she would ever get used to the idea that Nick loved her was another matter. But here in the circle of his arms, it felt entirely right. Her eyes made a loving study of that straight profile, the forceful jaw, the tow-coloured hair whose blondness almost matched her own. They would, she found herself thinking suddenly and dreamily, have *very* blond children. Then she realised that the grey eyes were watching her quizzically, under raised eyebrows.

'Do you think,' he asked drily, 'that you could stop studying me like a—like a shopper trying to decide whether to buy, and actually say yes?'

'Yes! If you're sure,' she said, with a sudden feeling of shyness.

'Haven't I been trying to convince you that I'm sure?' He kissed her swiftly, as if to give her added proof, and then said softly, '*Trust* me.'

'I do. I only didn't, because it all seemed to add up—' Kate looked at him sheepishly and then decided, rather quickly, not to raise the subject of *when* anything had happened. 'I've got eight months of my contract left to run,' she told him quickly.

'Have you? I've got fourteen months—it was a two-year one. You really like it, don't you?' he said, smiling at her. 'Working out here, coping with all the difficulties? The fascination's caught you, too. In spite of everything, somehow it *gets* you.'

'Yes, it does.' She decided not to remind him of his rude remarks when she'd first arrived because, after all, he had taken them back since then. All the same, he seemed to catch a glint of mischief in her eyes as she looked up at him, because he caught her to him again and kissed her hard, and dizzyingly, so that she had no breath for words. Then he said, as if it was all settled,

'We'll get married out here, then. And soon. I don't hold with long engagements. And no, not because of before! Much more because, with the hours we both work, we'd spend all our time having difficulties seeing each other, otherwise. And because I'd like to get you tied down before you can grow another crop of misunderstandings!'

He picked up the end of her plait and wound it round his hand, holding it up for her to see, making a gesture of her captivity with his eyes smouldering with laughter. And love. His words hadn't been a question, more of a command. All the same, Kate said meekly, and with her heart singing, 'Yes, Dr Kyle.'

'That's right, Staff Nurse—do as you're told.' But behind the laugh in his voice there was a deeper note, of passion, and promise. He said, softly, 'Honestly, my love, couldn't you see?'

'I'm—I'm not very good at *seeing*,' she told him, but one hand stole up to touch his cheek lovingly.

'Then I'll just have to keep on telling you, won't I?' He looked deep into her eyes, compelling her, filling her with warmth and a tingling knowledge of joy and completeness. *Nick*. Everything she had ever wanted. Everything she hadn't known she wanted, too. Challenge and danger and excitement as well as security.

'I love you, Cousin Kate,' he said.

'I love you too, Cousin Nick.'

'Then we've got nothing left to quarrel about, have we?' he asked, and picked up her hand to press it to his lips.

Another bouquet for the Rose of Romance.

A Highly Respectable Marriage by Sheila Walsh has won th[e]
1984 Romantic Novel of the Year award. Which only goes t[o]
prove, once again, that Mills and Boon are the leaders in
romantic fiction.

Award yourself a bouquet soon – A Highly Respectable
Marriage is available from 11th January 1985, price £1.50.

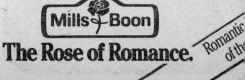

Mills ❀ Boon

The Rose of Romance.

Romantic
of th[e]

Mills & Boon

4 Doctor Nurse Romances
FREE

Coping with the daily tragedies and ordeals of a busy hospital, and sharing the satisfaction of a difficult job well done, people find themselves unexpectedly drawn together. Mills & Boon Doctor Nurse Romances capture perfectly the excitement, the intrigue and the emotions of modern medicine, that so often lead to overwhelming and blissful love. By becoming a regular reader of Mills & Boon Doctor Nurse Romances you can enjoy EIGHT superb new titles every two months plus a whole range of special benefits: your very own personal membership card, a free newsletter packed with recipes, competitions, bargain book offers, plus big cash savings.

AND an Introductory FREE GIFT for YOU,
Turn over the page for details.

Fill in and send this coupon back today
and we'll send you
4 Introductory
Doctor Nurse Romances yours to keep
FREE
At the same time we will reserve a
subscription to Mills & Boon
Doctor Nurse Romances for you. Every
two months you will receive the latest
8 new titles, delivered direct to your door.
You don't pay extra for delivery. Postage and
packing is always completely Free.
There is no obligation or commitment –
you receive books only for
as long as you want to.

It's easy! Fill in the coupon below and return it to
**MILLS & BOON READER SERVICE, FREEPOST, P.O. BOX 236,
CROYDON, SURREY CR9 9EL.**

Please note: **READERS IN SOUTH AFRICA** write to
Mills & Boon Ltd., Postbag X3010,
Randburg 2125, S. Africa.

- -

FREE BOOKS CERTIFICATE

**To: Mills & Boon Reader Service, FREEPOST, P.O. Box 236,
Croydon, Surrey CR9 9EL.**

Please send me, free and without obligation, four Dr. Nurse Romances, and reserve
Reader Service Subscription for me. If I decide to subscribe I shall receive, following my fr
parcel of books, eight new Dr. Nurse Romances every two months for £8.00, post a
packing free. If I decide not to subscribe, I shall write to you within 10 days. The free boo
are mine to keep in any case. I understand that I may cancel my subscription at any tir
simply by writing to you. I am over 18 years of age.
Please write in BLOCK CAPITALS.

Name _____

Address _____

_____

_____ Postcode _____

SEND NO MONEY — TAKE NO RISKS